"Do you have a girlfriend, Uncle Alex?"

Alex blinked in surprise.

Without answer "You should date M

Alex shook his that's a good idea."

The only problem was that part of him thought it *was* a good idea. The part that wasn't rational. The part that took risk for granted every time he climbed aboard the fire engine.

He needed to ignore that dangerous part as much as he needed to forget Chelsea's suggestion. As the adult, he needed to be sensible. He didn't know whether he'd accomplish that, but the one thing he knew for sure was that he wouldn't be able to get Dinah Fraser out of his mind.

* * *

Books by Dana Corbit

Love Inspired

A Blessed Life #188
An Honest Life #233
A New Life #274
A Family for Christmas #278
"Child in a Manger"
Christmas in the Air #322
"Season of Hope"
On the Doorstep #316
A Hickory Ridge Christmas #374
Little Miss Matchmaker #416

DANA CORBIT

has been fascinated with words since third grade, when she began stringing together stanzas of rhyme. That interest and an inherent nosiness led her to a career as a newspaper reporter and editor. After earning state and national recognition in journalism, she traded her career for stay-at-home motherhood.

But the need for creative expression followed her home, and later through the move from Indiana to Milford, Michigan. Outside the office, Dana discovered the joy of writing fiction. In stolen hours, between carpooling and church activities, she escapes into her private world, telling stories from her heart.

Dana makes her home in Michigan with her husband, three young daughters and two cats.

Little Miss Matchmaker
Dana Corbit

Steeple
Hill®

Published by Steeple Hill Books™

Special thanks and acknowledgment are given to Dana Corbit for her contribution to the A TINY BLESSINGS TALE miniseries.

STEEPLE HILL BOOKS

Steeple
Hill®

ISBN-13: 978-0-373-87452-1
ISBN-10:   0-373-87452-9

LITTLE MISS MATCHMAKER

www.SteepleHill.com

Printed in U.S.A.

The Lord is my light and my salvation; whom shall I fear? The Lord is the stronghold of my life; of whom should I be afraid?
—*Psalms* 27:1

To our youngest daughter, Alexa. I admire the way you see each day as an adventure, each unopened door as a mystery to be explored. May you always dream big and see the world for all it can be. Also to my friend, Elaine Heaton, who has faced this new twist in her life with such dignity and grace. My heart will follow you wherever you go in the world.

A special thanks to Mark Pehrson, our friend and veteran of the Novi (Michigan) Fire Department, for opening your world to me. You are a hero in every way.

Chapter One

If only everything were as easy to compartmental-ize, Alex thought as he stared at the wall of lockers. His own reflective jacket, bunker pants, boots and helmet were back in their proper places under the nameplate A. Donovan. Outside Station Four's gray brick walls, early October had already dressed Chest-nut Grove, Virginia, for autumn in its deepest reds and oranges, but Alex couldn't erase the scene he'd just left from his thoughts.

There would be no golden fall colors this year for the young family that had lived in the tiny house Engine Four had paid a visit to that morning. Only black, black and an unattractive gray.

The cruel irony of that loss of color ate at him when he needed to be praising God that there'd been no serious injuries or loss of life. That family had been blessed; he knew that. Even the family cat had made it out unscathed. Alex had pulled the terrified and hissing kitty out from under the bed himself.

Still, Alex imagined that it was hard for this family, already struggling and underinsured, to feel fortunate when they'd lost their furniture, family pictures and even the children's toys. At least they had memories, even if a lifetime of souvenirs had perished.

Some people weren't even fortunate enough to have memories—at least honest reflections that weren't based on a foundation of lies, he thought bitterly. Images of the day he'd discovered his adoption records entered his thoughts uninvited. His parents had carried the secret of his adoption to their graves rather than face him with the truth, and he would never forgive them for it.

Alex tucked the thoughts away the best he could as he trudged away from the lockers, past Engine Four and the utility truck, Squad Four, and into the back of the building. The only thing that mattered to him now was the shower to come. Perhaps the soap and water could wash away the funk in his heart along with the sweat and grime on his skin.

He was halfway up the stairs, halfway to his destination of steaming hot water and fresh-smelling soap, when a familiar voice rang out behind him.

"Hold up, Donovan."

Alex stopped on command, but he couldn't hold back a sigh as he turned to face Fire Chief Bill Nevins. The chief never liked to let too much time pass before analyzing his crew's performances on a run. Just this once, Alex wished Bill would let them recover before he began his analysis.

"You had a message in the office." Chief Nevins extended a pink note to Alex while still gripping a stack of his own messages in his other hand.

"Thanks." Alex returned to the landing and reached for the message, already uncomfortable though he didn't look at what it said right away. He didn't often receive messages at the station, and the last one he'd received had been bad enough news to make him dread the next.

"If memory serves, you might want to get on that message right away."

His boss's strange comment made him look down at the slip of paper in his hand. The feminine name at the top didn't ring any bells, but he recognized the location written beneath it: Grove Elementary School.

Chelsea? Was she all right? Had something happened at school? Had someone at the hospital made a mistake and called the school first instead of him? The questions were still pinging through his thoughts as he glanced up at his boss again. Bill wore a knowing smile.

"It hits hard and fast, doesn't it?"

"What's that?"

"The need to shelter and protect. That whole father thing."

Father thing? Alex shook his head to push aside the incredulous idea. He was no father, just a temporary guardian to two kids who had nowhere else to go. Not even a great guardian at that.

Still, he couldn't help looking back at the paper he held and backing away from the man who was getting a kick out of his discomfort. Written at the top of the sheet was "Dinah Fraser," whom he now remembered as the "Miss Fraser" that Chelsea spoke about in the evening over frozen-dinner lasagna or carryout roasted chicken. Even if he hadn't met her yet, Chelsea's teacher was one bit of stability in the child's otherwise out-of-control life.

"Don't worry. It's probably nothing," Bill told him, showing the decency that made him a good leader.

"Thanks." Turning, Alex headed down the hall instead of up the stairs as he'd planned. Inside the lounge was a partitioned area where firefighters could make personal calls either on their cell phones or the pay phone.

He dialed the number on the pay phone and waited, his heart pounding despite Bill's assurances.

"Grove Elementary School, how may I assist you?" said a voice so pleasant that the receptionist must have been smiling as she spoke.

"May I speak to Miss Fraser, please?"

"She's in class right now. May I put you through to her voice mail?"

Voice mail? Was she kidding? "No. I'm sorry, but I must speak to her right away." He managed to keep the agitation out of his voice, but there was no way he would hang up until he made sure everything was okay with Chelsea.

"But—" she began.

Alex cut her off. "This is Alex Donovan, Chelsea White's guardian. I'm returning Miss Fraser's call."

"Oh. I see."

Soon another line was ringing. And ringing. A feminine voice answered on the sixth ring.

"This is Miss Fraser."

"Hello. This is Alex Donovan."

"Oh, sorry it took me so long to get to the phone. We were outside conducting a diet soda and Mentos explosion experiment. It was so cool."

"Sounds like fun," he said because she seemed to expect it.

After a lengthy pause, she cleared her throat. "Thanks for returning my call. Yours came earlier than I expected."

He frowned at the phone. "Excuse me?"

"I told the receptionist to have you call after three."

"After three?" Alex looked down at the pink sheet still clutched in his hand. Sure enough, it said to call *after three.*

"Oh. Sorry." He didn't even bother to correct her that she'd spoken to the dispatcher at the station, not a receptionist. He'd made his own mistake by interrupting her class.

"Not a problem. I just wanted to set up a time to meet with you. I'm concerned about Chelsea."

Strange, the teacher had just suggested a problem, and Alex was breathing a sigh of relief. Chelsea was okay, at least physically. Her teacher was worried about her, but then so was he.

"How about after three this afternoon?"

Her question brought him back into the conversation with a start.

"Oh, yeah. That's when you get out of school."

Suddenly, the background noise of boisterous kids came through the line. He must have filtered it out before while anxiously awaiting what she had to say. By now her students must have been hanging from the fluorescent lights and taking turns leaping from the teacher's desk.

"This afternoon will be great, if you're not too busy. Sorry again for the interruption."

"It's fine. Really."

Alex glanced at his watch as he stood up from the desk and hurried upstairs. He needed to get moving if he planned to shower before he visited Grove Elementary, and showering wasn't optional unless he wanted to meet Chelsea's teacher smelling like a campfire gone bad.

So much for the long steamy shower he'd planned, to wash away his frustration from this morning along with the soot. He wasn't forgetting that young family's problems, but he and his relatives had some problems of their own right now. For his cousin Karla's sake, he was going to find a way to help her daughter cope.

Alex felt like a giant in a dollhouse as he walked through the halls of Grove Elementary School, passing low-set drinking fountains and artwork displayed far below his eye level. After a few wrong turns in the maze of hallways, he reached Room Twenty-three. A colorful display of artwork made from autumn leaves covered the partially closed door.

Knocking, Alex popped his head inside, looking around for the teacher's desk. Of course she wasn't sitting at it. He was more than fifteen minutes late. He would probably have left, himself, if someone made him wait that long.

But just as he started to back out of the room, the

door to a storage closet behind the desk closed, revealing an auburn-haired beauty standing behind it. Her eyes were as blue as the buttoned sweater she wore with a simple black skirt.

Alex knew he should look away—it was rude not to—but he just couldn't pull his gaze away from the woman who stared back at him. She'd tried her best, but even in her prim schoolteacher outfit, she couldn't hide her feminine curves.

Okay, he'd had an unfair picture of what a third-grade teacher might look like. *Pixie* came to mind. Even *matronly.* He remembered plenty of teachers like that from his own school days. But *captivating?* He'd certainly never expected to find a woman who looked like that at Grove Elementary.

A woman who just happened to be Chelsea's teacher, he reminded himself when she cleared her throat and glanced down at the black toes of her shoes. Great, now Miss Fraser probably thought that he was some kind of creep.

"Miss Fraser?" he asked in a voice that barely resembled his own.

"Mr. Donovan?" But as if she'd answered her own question, she gestured toward her desk. "Come in. Have a seat. And please call me Dinah."

Funny, calling her by her first name sounded like a really bad idea when "Miss Fraser" or something even more distant like "Miss Chelsea's Teacher" might be better.

Still, he found himself nodding at her suggestion. "Call me Alex."

He gripped her hand—another mistake—and retreated to the other side of her desk, pulling up a too-short chair from one of the desks. The tingling in his fingers probably had nothing to do with the woman seated across from him and everything to do with the subject they were about to discuss. That she smiled then and left him distracted was beside the point. Dinah—make that Miss Fraser—was probably used to having that kind of effect on men.

"Thank you for coming, especially on such short notice."

"It's for Chelsea," he said because it really was as simple as that.

"Chelsea and Brandon are blessed to have you as their guardian."

Blessed was a strong word, but Alex thanked her, anyway.

Settling back in her chair and crossing her arms, Dinah squinted her eyes as if deep in thought. "You're Chelsea's 'Uncle Alex.' Are you her mother's brother or her father's brother?"

"Technically, Karla and I are cousins." Not even that if they were talking about blood relatives, but he didn't mention that. "But the two of us have always been more like brother and sister. Chelsea and Brandon are like my niece and nephew."

Dinah had a strange look on her face, as if what he'd said had surprised her. "As I said, Chelsea's a blessed little girl."

Alex cleared his throat. What was he supposed to say to that?

"But she's also a very troubled girl," she added.

"Can you blame her?" He shrugged and lowered his gaze to the floor. "As if it wasn't bad enough that her dad's a Marine rooting out insurgents in Iraq, now her mom's in a Philadelphia cancer-treatment center undergoing intense chemotherapy."

"She's had an awful lot to deal with," she agreed.

Dinah was studying him when he looked up at her again, suggesting that she was including him in her compassionate comment. Alex stiffened. He didn't want her pity. Opening his guest bedrooms, juggling a few schedules and learning to make something edible out of frozen chicken breasts couldn't come close to comparing to what Brandon and Chelsea had been facing.

"Everything's going to be okay, though. Karla's husband, Mike, is trying to get leave soon, and Karla will be just fine." Even as he said it, Alex wondered which of them he was trying to convince.

"You just keep reassuring Chelsea of that at home, and I'll do the same here at school."

"How is she doing in school?" The question sounded strange in his ears. He'd always figured that one day he would attend parent-teacher conferences, but this wasn't at all how he would have imagined it.

"That's just the thing. Her grades are as high as they were last year."

"Last year?"

"Our principal likes to loop second- and third-grade classes, so the children benefit from the stability of spending two years with the same teacher and the same classmates. Next year, Chelsea will go on to a new teacher, and I'll start with a new group of second-graders."

Stability. For the second time that day, Alex was thankful Chelsea had it at school if she couldn't have it anywhere else. But it was also strange to realize that this Dinah Fraser, a stranger to him, probably knew the child he adored better than he did.

"So it's not her grades?"

She shook her head. "She's just so withdrawn and depressed. It's as if all the sunshine has been lifted out of her eyes."

That was it. As much as he'd known there was something different about Chelsea, he hadn't been able to describe it. Dinah's description had put his thoughts into words.

"In class, she's so distracted that I had to move her desk away from the window to get her to pay attention," she continued. "Still, I can barely get her to participate in classroom activities."

Dinah planted her elbows on her desk and rested her chin in the V formed by her hands. "She used to make all this beautiful artwork, and now she doesn't even want to color. She let herself be eliminated from the class Spelling Bee in the first round when I know full well she remembered that the *e* comes before the *i* in *receive*. You know, that *i* before *e* except after *c*…"

She stopped herself when she glanced up and caught him grinning at her. Shrugging, she smiled back at him. It was obvious that Miss Fraser loved teaching, and she was proving by this meeting that she loved her students, as well. If he'd ever had a teacher like her, maybe his own academic records would have leaned closer to the beginning of the alphabet instead of a few letters in.

He must have looked at her a little too long because Dinah blushed prettily and glanced away. Dinah Fraser might be used to getting more than her share of male attention, but that didn't mean she was comfortable with it. She would have laughed if she'd realized that at least this time his thoughts weren't on her appearance at all.

Still, he wondered how he could have lived in the area a whole year without ever meeting her.

"Fraser. I've heard that name before around here. Do you have relatives in Chestnut Grove?"

"Yes, there are a lot of us around."

When she didn't elaborate, Alex figured it was time to quit procrastinating. No matter how out of character it was for him, he needed to ask this woman for help.

"So…ah…what suggestions do you have for helping Chelsea outside of school?"

"Does Chelsea talk about her mom at home?"

He shrugged, frustration replacing his earlier discomfort at asking for help. "Not much. In fact not at all unless Karla's just called, and even then it's just to say that her mom says hi and she's doing fine."

"It might help her to talk more about her mother's illness or the danger her dad's facing, or both. She could even keep a journal, writing down feelings."

Alex frowned. He'd known she shouldn't keep her feelings bottled up, but he felt powerless trying to help her. "She doesn't seem to want to talk about it."

"You know there's a difference between want and need. She needs to talk about her feelings, and if she won't initiate the conversations, you might have to. Either that or I can have her talk to the school counselor."

"No, that's okay." *Counselor.* He didn't even like the sound of that word. It was bad enough asking the teacher for help, but asking some professional counselor would be like admitting failure. Like admitting he couldn't handle the situation when he'd promised Karla he would.

Instead of arguing for counseling as he expected— he'd always thought that women single-handedly financed the counseling industry—she nodded. "Be prepared, though. There might be a lot of tears when she finally opens up."

Alex shivered at the notion. "You sure know how to kill a guy."

"Where is Chelsea now?"

Alex glanced at his watch. "She'd be off the bus now. My next-door neighbor stays with Brandon and Chelsea until I get home from work. I know it isn't a perfect situation."

"You're doing the best you can. It has to be good enough."

He doubted that whatever he did would be good enough. But she was right. He was doing the best he could. He'd had to call in favors from all of his fellow firefighters to even be able to temporarily pull weekday eight-to-five shifts when usual shifts were twenty-four hours on and forty-eight off. He didn't know how long he could expect his coworkers to make concessions for him so he could care for his cousin's children.

"How's Brandon doing with having a babysitter?"

"He doesn't fight me too much on it anymore, not since I told him the sitter was really for Chelsea. It's about the only thing he doesn't fight me on lately."

"Sounds like a normal teenager."

Alex frowned. He didn't have a clue what normal teenagers did, and he barely remembered his own teen years.

"You've had an introduction to parenting by fire."

"What do you mean?" he asked, cocking his head.

"Oh." She straightened, drawing her hands into her lap. "I guess I just assumed this was your first parenting experience. Since you weren't…uh…wearing a wedding ring or anything. But I guess I shouldn't assume…anything nowadays…."

Dinah let her words fall away, her blush deepening with each of her awkward comments. The familiar need to protect and preserve filled Alex, and he didn't even have on his gear. He hated making her feel this uncomfortable even if he was secretly pleased that she'd admitted to checking his hand for a wedding band.

"Assume away. I don't have any little Alexes running around anywhere. I'm a bit traditional when it comes to the marriage-before-kids order of things. And I've never done the first, so…"

She nodded as he let his words fall away, but her cheeks were still stained pink.

His gaze lowered to her hand again, where she wore nothing more significant than a thin gold pinkie ring. Her title had given him the heads-up that she was unmarried, but he still was surprised that she didn't even wear an engagement ring. She probably had to dodge proposals left and right.

"Then we're even," she said finally.

"Even?"

"No kids."

"At least you have some training with them."

She smiled. "Nothing like the on-the-job variety you're getting."

"Training," he said, scoffing at her comment. "I guess you could call it that. But usually in on-the-job training you have a supervisor to tell you if you're doing things wrong. I hope I'm not messing these kids up forever."

"They'll be fine." She paused long enough to give him a smile that could warm the North Pole by a few degrees. "Kids are resilient and forgiving, just like hostas. Ever planted a hosta?"

She must have seen his incredulous look because she explained. "Hostas are really hardy perennials. Pretty much no matter what you do to them, they'll still come back in the spring."

"So if your analogy holds true, Chelsea and Brandon will survive no matter what I do to—"

She was shaking her head before he'd presented the whole premise. "The theory need not be tested." But she smiled as she said it.

"Good. Do I look like the kind of man who might grow hostas?" He raised his hand as a sign to stop her. "Wait. Don't answer that. My masculinity might be bruised."

"Probably not. You didn't strike me as the green-thumbed type."

"What type did I strike you as?" He took an unhurried look at her, waiting for her to glance away. For the longest time she didn't, and it surprised him how dry his mouth was by the time she did.

"Don't answer that, either," he said to diffuse the electrical charge filling the air. Even a fire hose couldn't douse that spark.

"You struck me as Chelsea's very important guardian."

So much for the charge. He couldn't decide whether she'd said it for his sake or hers, but either way, she was right. His plate was already overfilled with his temporary family. The last thing he needed was to let a beautiful woman distract him from the all-important job of caring for Chelsea and Brandon.

Besides, he'd avoided female complications for the last year and the plan was working for him, so he didn't want to mess that up by letting a pretty redhead turn his head.

From now on he would see Miss Fraser—yes, it was better to think of her that way—only as a partner in helping Chelsea get through this tough time. He wouldn't allow himself to be attracted to the lovely teacher with the sweet disposition.

That was final. *Finito.* So why did he feel as if it was a little late for him to be making that decision—like running into a blaze when there was nothing left but smoldering embers?

Chapter Two

Dinah watched as Alex strode out of her classroom, all muscle and sinew—proof of a man who regularly put his back into his work. A sigh escaped her before she knew it was coming. Even as she pulled her gaze away from his retreating form—from the pale yellow polo shirt that stretched across his back as he moved—her cheeks burned.

Since when did she notice broad shoulders, toned biceps or even deep brown eyes and neatly trimmed dark hair when the only thing that truly mattered about a person lay deep inside him where no one but God could see? What mattered was his heart.

A small smile settled on her lips. That argument wouldn't work when Alex Donovan appeared to be just as appealing on the inside as he was outside where the rest of the world could see. And the world had to see unless all the people in it had simultaneously closed their eyes. Still, what other bachelor could she name who would drop everything in his life and step in to care for a cousin's children when he had none of his own?

Her brother, Jonah? She shook her head as she flipped open her grade book and glanced down at the list of names and corresponding scores for spelling and geography tests and daily math homework. Jonah was a great guy. He'd even served his country and fought for freedom in Iraq, but he would probably draw the line when it came to becoming guardian to someone else's kids. She wouldn't have put it past him to recommend her for the job, though.

Okay, there was one other man she knew of who might have done something that extreme in his bachelor days, but then her father had always stood head and shoulders above other men in her opinion.

What did that say about Alex Donovan? That he was brave? He did fight fires for a living, and most cowards probably avoided that high-risk career like a case of leprosy. Did it say he was a loving person then? She had only to see the way that Chelsea talked about her "Uncle Alex" to know that one was true.

Dinah stopped herself before she applied every desirable personality trait her amazing father possessed to Alex, the majority of which she couldn't possibly confirm or discount.

You struck me as Chelsea's very important guardian. She reminded herself of her own words that she'd used to cut off his flirting. He had been flirting, too. She might not have been a true veteran of the dating wars, but she'd been in enough minor skirmishes to know that one for sure.

If she were honest with herself, she would have to admit she hadn't discouraged him initially, but she decided to attribute that to the shock of seeing a massive, gorgeous man in her classroom when the males who surrounded her most days stood about waist high. Sure, she'd scheduled the three o'clock appointment with a grown-up, but this was her excuse, and she was sticking to it.

"What kind of daydreams are you having?"

Dinah jerked her head toward the sound, finding kindergarten teacher Shelley Foust standing in the doorway to her classroom, her arms crossed and a knowing expression on her face.

"What do you mean?" Dinah did her best to act nonchalant as she closed the grade book she hadn't been looking at anyway.

"You know what I mean. Tall, dark and hunky who just walked out of this room, his shoulders barely fitting through the doorway."

For a brand-new teacher, straight from Penn State, Shelley didn't miss much, especially the interesting stories at Grove Elementary. "Just try to tell me you didn't notice."

Dinah opened her mouth to try and then closed it again, remembering how her mother and father taught her that lying was sinful. She cleared her throat. "Oh, him? That was just Alex Donovan, Chelsea White's guardian while her mom is undergoing cancer treatment."

Shelley stepped farther into the room and brushed away the wrinkles on her darling prairie skirt and fitted blouse. Everything looked effortlessly cute on the petite kindergarten teacher, and sometimes Dinah had to try not to envy that when she always struggled to find clothes modest enough for her too-curvy figure.

"I doubt that man could be called *just* anything, but whatever you say," Shelley said. "Now I need details. Age. Occupation. Marital status."

Dinah frowned at her but still relented. "Thirtysomething if I were to guess." Those crinkles around his eyes had given her a clue. "Firefighter."

Shelley rubbed her hands together. "Ooh, I just knew he would be something manly like that. I was leaning toward construction worker or forester from the National Park Service or something, but I can picture him now rushing into burning buildings or rescuing kittens from trees."

Because she could see it, too, Dinah turned her attention to the dry-erase board at the other side of her classroom. She would need to clean that and jot down tomorrow's assignments before she left for the night.

"What about that last, all-important detail?"

"Oh, that. He's single."

Why was it that she wanted to be able to tell Shelley that Alex was married with a half-dozen children and a set of twins on the way? If a little forward, Shelley wasn't a danger to local single men. She'd dated only a few since the beginning of the school year and was always kind when she ended a relationship. For some reason, though, Dinah hoped her friend didn't set her sights on Chelsea's kind guardian.

"But taken?" Shelley lifted a delicate brow when she glanced back at her.

Dinah shook her head. "I only met him today, but he did seem awfully busy working and caring for his cousin's two children right now. Probably too busy for a lot of socializing." He'd found time for a few minutes of it with her, but Dinah didn't mention that.

Though Shelley nodded, she didn't appear convinced.

Dinah's cheeks burned as realization dawned. "You mean me? I told you I just met him during a conference about Chelsea."

"You certainly know a lot of his *details*."

"Because we were discussing the difficult situation that Chelsea's in." Maybe it wasn't necessary for her to know his personal value regarding marriage and children, but that was beside the point.

"Whatever you say." Shelley still didn't sound convinced, but then she sighed. "You're probably right. The fabulous firefighter would be too busy right now to spoil me properly, so I guess I won't be asking you to introduce us."

It was Dinah's turn to lift an eyebrow. "You're sure?"

"You know how I expect to be spoiled when I date someone."

Though she knew nothing of the sort, Dinah nodded. She sensed that her friend might be stepping aside for her sake, and she should let Shelley know the gesture was unnecessary, but she couldn't speak up.

It was probably for the best. Alex's life was complicated enough without Dinah introducing him to the spunky kindergarten teacher. She was probably doing him a favor by not giving him another distraction.

Whether he would see her sacrifice as a favor or not,

she wouldn't have to find out since she didn't plan to tell him. She also wouldn't have to confess to feeling relief that the firefighter she barely knew and shouldn't be planning to get to know better wouldn't be meeting someone else.

Ross Van Zandt set a heavy file box next to the sofa, leaning back into the cushions without opening it. He could have worked in his office this afternoon, but he preferred to be home as much as he could these days.

He reached for the remote control and flipped on daytime television, not expecting quality viewing but still looking for white noise. As if to confirm his prediction, a local celebrity's face appeared on the screen in an extreme close-up.

"Good afternoon, Richmond. I'm Douglas Matthews, and I would like to welcome you to *Afternoons with Douglas Matthews*."

"How many more times can he cram Douglas Matthews into one sentence?" Ross grumbled.

As the camera pulled away, the black-haired and blue-eyed talk show host leaned in and smiled with unnaturally white teeth, as if he was talking to his best friends. All half a million or so of his buddies outside the screen.

"You're going to love our lineup today. First up, is your garden ready for the snowy season? Our garden expert will offer the Top Ten tips for planting, pruning and primping to ensure a plentiful spring."

Ross rolled his eyes as he opened the box at his feet. The talk show host prattled on about how to make marinated salmon with some local celebrity or other, but Ross tuned out the rest.

Why did people watch that garbage, anyway? *Afternoons* didn't deal with anything meatier than the best food for roses or favorite boat tours on Richmond's Kanawha Canal.

From what Ross had heard, Matthews had made a scene at the Starlight Diner when *Richmond Gazette* reporter Jared Kierney had suggested a show on the Tiny Blessings adoption scandal. Even if Matthews didn't want to help people by sharing their stories, at least Ross would have expected the talk show host to jump on the story for a ratings boost. With material like today's lineup, he probably needed it.

"You've procrastinated long enough, Van Zandt." Ross blew out a breath as he forced his attention back to the box of records.

He knew this drill. For the last two months he'd been going through these records systematically, comparing them to the documents on file at Tiny Blessings and trying to weed out the truth from an overgrowth of lies. He was glad he could provide pro bono private investigative services for the agency his wife headed because Tiny Blessings would never be able to afford those services otherwise.

At the squeak on the stairs, Ross was sorry he'd

decided to leave the office and pore over more records at home today. Kelly didn't need any more aggravation these days, and this newest crisis facing the agency was nothing if not aggravating.

Just when they thought they'd put the scandal involving illegal adoptions behind them, more falsified records had been discovered in the walls of the Harcourt mansion during the renovation project by Ben Cavanaugh's construction company.

Ross had hoped Kelly would relinquish more of the responsibility, and the headaches that went along with it, to Eric Pellegrino, the agency's new assistant director she'd hired to take the pressure off her pregnancy. But he knew Kelly better than that. For all the crises and bad publicity the agency faced, his wife believed the buck stopped with her.

The woman he loved appeared then at the end of the sofa, her hands resting on her rounded belly, her hair mussed from a nap.

"I thought you were supposed to be resting."

Kelly frowned at him and then lowered herself on the sofa cushion. "I'm too tired to sleep, but I'm sure I won't be sleeping tonight, either. Our little acrobat likes choosing that for gym time."

Still, she gave her stomach a loving pat. "This counts as resting. I'll even put my feet up if you scoot over."

Ross did as he was told, as all husbands of extremely pregnant wives should do for their self-protection. Tucking a pillow beneath her feet that she had settled on the brown leather ottoman, he reached in the box and pulled out a stack of files.

"Who are we looking at today?" she asked, holding out a hand for him to offer her a stack.

"I just thought I would flip through these again. Maybe this time a name will ring a bell."

"I hate thinking that some of these adoptive children searching for their birth parents will never find the answers they're looking for though we have the answers right here."

"With a lot of work and even more prayer, we'll help them find those answers," he told her.

Ross scooted closer to his wife, propped his feet next to hers and glanced down at the names on the file tabs.

"Bailey-Brock-Brown," he read aloud. "Brown? If that won't be like finding a needle in a haystack." Every single name in those case files was another needle, but neither of them needed a reminder of that.

"Daley-Davenport-Dexter," Kelly read aloud from her own pile before looking over at him.

Ross shook his head. "No. Nothing."

"Yeah, me, neither."

They continued on, listing names back and forth, but none sounded familiar. Even if one had, it wouldn't have made a difference since these could have been the mothers' maiden names—if these were the real files and not just another round of doctored documents.

Ross stopped on a file that said "Harcourt."

"Now there's a familiar name." He turned the tab to the side, letting Kelly take a look. "I wonder how many Harcourt offspring are running around Chestnut Grove and the rest of Virginia without any idea who they really are."

"Maybe a few. As long as the young women's parents were willing to pay for Barnaby Harcourt's silence. I doubt he gave relatives a discount on his rates." Kelly frowned as she always did when she mentioned the founding director of Tiny Blessings whose illegal acts had tarnished the agency's reputation.

For curiosity's sake as much as anything, Ross flipped open the file and started calculating.

"This baby's a thirty-three-year-old man now. Birth mother is named Cynthia. Recognize that one?"

She shook her head. "And her last name could be anything now."

"The father is listed as 'unknown.'"

Kelly made a sound of acknowledgment in her throat but didn't comment further. The absence of a birth father was as common an occurrence in the adoption-agency business as the lack of complete information.

Ross's hands tightened on the folder. If he couldn't solve the problems for the agency his wife loved, then he'd at least hoped to help her reunite some of the adoptive children with their birth parents. Even in that plan, he was failing Kelly.

Shuffling the papers again, he smacked the file closed, but when he did, something fell to the ground. It wasn't much, just a tiny slip of yellowing paper, about the size of a sticky note.

Ross automatically reached down to grab it and stuff it back in the file, but the two words stopped him with his hand still held high: "See Donovan."

He cleared his throat, his pulse pounding. "Honey, ever see this?"

"What is it?" she asked, but her eyes widened and she reached into the box between them.

It was all Ross could do not to shove his pregnant wife out of the way and start riffling in the box himself, but somehow he managed to wait until she was finished. Her frown didn't leave any doubt that she hadn't found the file, but her expression lifted again, and she tilted her head to the side.

"You don't think—"

"No," he blurted. He didn't need her to finish to know how crazy the idea sounded. It was too easy. He'd been a P.I. long enough to know it was never that easy.

But what if it is? an unwelcome voice inside him suggested. Maybe just this once, a case could be as simple as someone forgetting to remove a note from a file that the owner never intended anyone to find.

Ross glanced across the room, his gaze landing on two more boxes of files next to the breakfast bar. Kelly had been bringing them home frequently, cross-checking files from the office with the duplicates found inside the wall at the Harcourt mansion.

"You don't happen to have any more *D*s, do you?"

"I think so," she said, already trying to push herself off the couch.

"Here, let me get it."

He couldn't get to the box fast enough. It was the thrill of the chase, and he knew it well. He flipped through the files, his hands landing on one that said "Donovan." He carried it back to the couch, so they could look at it together.

"It might not even be the same Donovan," he said to keep his own hopes from getting too high.

As he opened the file, his gaze, well trained from looking at so many documents, went right to the date of birth.

"It's a match."

That they'd both said it at the same time made them laugh, but they stopped just as quickly. Okay, they had a match. Now what?

Ross flipped through the file, reading about George and Edie Donovan and the newborn infant they adopted and named Alex. This version listed the birth mother as Mary Something-or-other, but it was probably the bogus one.

He handed the file to Kelly, already planning his steps. First, he would do an Internet search for the Donovans' son, and then he would start eliminating from that pool those who couldn't be this particular guy. Part of him hated to mess up another person's well-ordered life, but the man deserved the chance to know the truth.

For a long time, Kelly didn't look up from the file. She simply stared at it as if willing it to complete the puzzle. She leaned her head to one shoulder and to the other as if considering, and finally she turned back to him.

"Isn't Eli Cavanaugh's friend, the fireman who moved from Richmond, named Alex Donovan?"

"Hey, Donovan, get out here and shoot some hoops with us," Trent Gillman called from the court adjacent to the parking lot as Alex climbed out of his SUV.

"Give me a few." Alex shut the door and started toward the station. Basketball was one of the ways the men and women at the station killed a few hours on slow days or burned off steam after busier or more stressful ones. Today had certainly been one of the more stressful variety.

"Make it quick. We need somebody to kill in three-on-three." To make his point, Trent drove by Cory Long for a perfect layup and then lifted his arms in a Rocky-style victory dance.

"You mean you need me to let you win?"

When a ball came sailing toward him, Alex ducked inside the gray brick structure through the side door.

He traded his khaki pants and polo shirt for a hooded sweatshirt and loose-fitting warm-ups and jogged back outside to join the game. Already, several firefighters, including Fire Chief Nevins, were taking shots.

"Think fast."

Alex shot his hands up to his face in time to catch the ball aimed at his head. "Thanks, man."

"No problem," Trent said.

On the court, Alex executed a perfect chest shot. "You see boys, nothin' but net." Going in for the rebound, he balanced the ball on his right hand, setting up for a shot with his left.

"How was your afternoon with the preacher's daughter?" Trent asked just as Alex took the shot.

No net this time, the ball bounced off the backboard with a thud and then dropped into the grass. Alex turned back to him, drawing his eyebrows together. "What are you talking about? I don't know any preacher's daughter. I was just at a conference with Chelsea's teacher."

"You mean Miss Fraser? Miss Dinah Fraser?"

"Daughter of Reverend John Fraser," Bill Nevins filled in the blank when Alex turned his perplexed expression on him.

Fraser, of course. He'd met Reverend Fraser of Chestnut Grove Community Church, a few times during last year's Community holiday toy drive.

It was strange, though, that when he'd asked Dinah about her common surname, she hadn't even mentioned her well-known father. She'd said only that there were a lot of Frasers around. What was that all about? It had been difficult enough for him to picture someone like Dinah as an elementary teacher, but a preacher's daughter? That just didn't seem possible.

"Puts a whole new spin on the lovely Miss Fraser, doesn't it?" Trent said.

Cory, who hadn't spoken up until then, snickered.

Alex wheeled on his coworkers. It didn't matter that Trent had only voiced Alex's thoughts. He didn't feel like cutting his tactless friend a little slack the way he usually did. Today even the fact that he had a good heart might not keep Trent from landing on his backside.

"Have a death wish, Gillman?" Bill asked, before Alex had the chance. "Then I wouldn't say another word about *the lady*." He put enough emphasis on the last two words to show he meant business.

After a few strange glances among the other firefighters, the subject fell away, leaving only six guys and a round orange ball to fill the void. Alex jumped higher, dribbled faster and guarded more aggressively than he had in a long time. That Trent happened to get fouled a few extra times—in the pursuit of the game, of course—couldn't be avoided.

Alex couldn't explain his need to defend a woman he barely knew, but there it was. As much as he would like to believe he would rush to protect any woman's honor, he wondered if he would be as forceful in every case.

When the game ended, all six men poured off the court, drenched and a little bruised. The chief looked more winded than most as he came up behind Alex and rested a hand on his shoulder.

"Some game, wasn't it?" Alex said, resisting the urge to shake his boss's hand off his shoulder. His arm was sore, and he was regretting his "enthusiasm" in the game.

Bill made an affirmative grunt and rubbed his elbow where he had battled tendonitis over the years. "There's only one thing I can say, Donovan."

"What's that?"

"That must have been *some* conference with Miss Dinah Fraser."

Chapter Three

Dinah startled in her seat as the fire alarm squawked in deafening, repetitive bursts. As if the alarm signaled the beginning of chaos rather than an announcement for safety, a clamor broke out in the classroom around her.

"Everyone, please be quiet," she said in a loud stage whisper. "It's probably only a fire drill." At least she hoped it was, though she hadn't received advance warning of a scheduled drill.

Dinah set aside the copy of *The Secret Garden* that she'd been reading to the class and grabbed her grade book. She would need that to check attendance once they reached their designated meeting place by the curb.

"Now let's line up by the door. I want everyone to stay in line and be silent until we're past the flagpole."

At a lower level of chaos, her twenty-four students followed her down the corridor to the side entry. Just as she reached the flagpole, two fire engines and two smaller trucks that must have been for paramedics came roaring up the street toward the school, lights flashing and sirens blaring. When all four trucks stopped, two firefighters, dressed in full gear, including helmets, climbed down from one of the fire engines and entered the building through the front door.

Definitely not a drill. Dinah's chest tightened, and as she glanced back to the children and then at the building behind them, she hoped her smile didn't falter.

She switched from the front of the line to the rear so when they all turned an about-face, she could lead her students back into the classroom. It also put her between the children she adored and the building in the unlikely case this was a real fire.

All around them, other classes poured out of the building, some well controlled and others as chaotic as Dinah's had been. Some classes had stopped to grab jackets, but most of the students were shivering and fidgeting to keep warm. High-pitched voices chatted about the supposed causes of a fire and the amount of time until recess.

Dinah scanned down the names in her grade book— from Austin Carlyle to Lily Polson to Kellan Stolz. As always she felt a twinge of nervousness until she'd made certain that all of her students stood with her on terra firma.

When her gaze fell to Chelsea White's name, she looked back to the fire engines. Though all four trucks were still parked in front of the school, most of the fire-fighters remained inside them. Was Alex Donovan one of the men in the truck, or maybe one of those still in the building? Not that she really cared or anything. She was only curious, and he happened to be the only firefighter she knew in Chestnut Grove.

Still, her cheeks and neck warmed at the thought of him, an unfortunate reaction she'd experienced too frequently these last few days, even more problematic since she thought of him so often.

Dinah shrugged. No matter what she thought and even no matter that they'd made a connection of sorts in their first meeting, the handsome firefighter would probably lose interest the minute he discovered from which branch of the Fraser family tree she'd sprung.

The alarm stopped blaring as suddenly as it had started. Another false alarm. There had already been three since school started. Someone had probably pulled it again and was standing out here, just as cold and miserable as everyone else but now holding a secret, too.

For the next few minutes, they all stood shivering and waiting for the bell that would signal their permission to return to the building. Dinah was so focused on the school entrance as she waited for the firefighters to exit through it that she didn't notice the other firefighter who approached from behind her and touched her sweater-clad arm.

"Hey there, Miss Fraser."

She didn't need to see his face to know who was there. His familiar voice felt like a warm caress sliding up her neck, and her arm tingled where he'd touched it. The sensation surprised her because she'd thought her skin was too numb to feel anything.

Still, when she turned to face him, she did her best

to appear surprised. Already a large man, Alex appeared massive wearing bunker pants and a cumbersome tan jacket with reflective bands on its chest, bottom edge and sleeves. He must have left his helmet in the truck.

"Oh, Mr. Donovan, it's good to see you again." She cleared her throat. "I mean…well, the circumstances aren't the best, but—"

"I know what you mean."

She smiled, grateful he'd saved her from whatever inane thing she would have said if she'd had time to come up with one. "Sorry about the false alarm."

"Yeah, me, too."

"We've had a few lately."

His nod and his frown combined. "It's unfortunate and not just because it's illegal to trigger a false alarm. If you have a lot of false alarms, people begin to not take them seriously."

It was Dinah's turn to frown. She'd worried about that exact thing. "You don't mean…"

He shook his head as he must have picked up on her meaning. "No, the fire department responds every time as though it's a real emergency. Even to those locations where there's a bad track record."

Dinah grimaced. Her school certainly had one of those.

But instead of criticizing as he had every right to, Alex waved away the situation as water under the bridge.

"What can you do?" he said with a sigh as he scanned the rows of students. "Since I was here anyway, I thought I would come over and say hello to my best girl."

Dinah swallowed hard, and her neck tingled before

she had the chance to really process what he'd said. Best girl? Did guys in the New Millennium still use an old term like that? Maybe they did when they were referring to a child who looked up to them with adoration in her huge, light brown eyes.

Chelsea was doing just that when Dinah caught the tiny blonde's approach in her side vision. The child's cap of straight, chin-length hair blew every which way, and her long-sleeved T-shirt probably wasn't keeping her warm, but Chelsea still grinned like a child on Christmas morning as she stared at her hero.

Best girl. Of course. It humiliated Dinah to admit that, just for a second, she'd wished Alex had been talking about her. Who could blame the little girl for some hero adoration over Alex when Dinah had a mild case of that herself, and she was nowhere near a child.

"Hi, Uncle Alex," Chelsea said almost shyly as she stepped closer to him.

"Get over here, you goofy kid." Alex bent at the waist and held his hands wide.

That wouldn't have been Dinah's choice for what to say to a child, but the petite nine-year-old grinned and ran into his arms. So much for what she knew.

"Did you come here to put out the fire?" Chelsea asked him when she pulled back.

"There's no fire. It's a false alarm."

"Oh." The child stared back at the building and nodded as if just realizing that it wouldn't be burning to the ground today.

"But you should always react to an alarm as if there could be a real fire," he reminded her.

"Okay."

Dinah couldn't help but smile at that. Alex was so worried about being an inadequate guardian, and already Chelsea accepted his direction without question. Sometimes she would have given anything to have that kind of authority in the classroom.

"What are you smiling about?"

Alex lifted an eyebrow when Dinah turned after hearing his question. His bare hands must have been cold because he stuffed them in the pockets of his jacket.

When he might have looked away, he continued to watch her. His intelligent eyes seemed to see right through her, to recognize the loneliness in her that she'd always tried to hide. She wasn't used to feeling this exposed, and yet for the life of her, she couldn't look away.

If not for the bell that rang, signaling the all clear and making her leap back at least four inches, she might have gone right on staring back at him. Alex seemed to look away reluctantly, as well.

As if they both remembered where they were at the same time, Alex and Dinah glanced down at Chelsea. The two of them hadn't been the only ones staring the last few minutes, and the child's knowing smile hinted at just what she'd seen. Chelsea looked back and forth between them, her smile widening. If Alex really had been able to look into Dinah's eyes and sense her thoughts, maybe Chelsea shared that family trait.

Dinah cleared her throat and turned to the rest of the class. "Okay, everyone. It's time to go back inside. Please keep quiet and stay in line until we reach the classroom."

"Well, I'd better get back to the truck. See you tonight, kiddo." Alex gave Chelsea one last hug.

"Good seeing you, Mr. Donovan."

Dinah started forward, putting on an air of nonchalance that she hoped Alex would buy. She couldn't remember ever being around a man who put her nerve endings on alert the way he did. Her palms were so damp that she would be embarrassed if one of her students took her hand on the way inside the building. Despite her best resistance, she glanced over her shoulder at Alex, hoping he wouldn't catch her.

He did, and he smiled and waved. "Goodbye, Miss Fraser. Tell Reverend Fraser I said hello."

Dinah swallowed. If he knew about her family, why had he pretended not to the other day? But she had no time to process the information, not when she had twenty-four students behind her, who all needed to return to their classroom. Their chatter followed her inside the building and down the hall, but she didn't take time to correct them.

She had a job to do, had a class full of third-graders relying on her to restore order and to make them feel safe at school, and she wouldn't let anything, even her own hormones, get in the way of her doing it.

Soon, she'd taken her place behind her desk, and the students were back at their own grouped desks working on the illustrations for their personal narratives as they had been before the alarm. Dinah had just opened her copy of *The Secret Garden* again, when Chelsea raised her hand. Dinah would have been annoyed with the interruption, but at least the child was participating in class again.

"Yes, Chelsea? Do you need help with something?"

Chelsea nodded, as if she had a serious matter to discuss. Dinah straightened in her chair. She wasn't sure what she would say if Chelsea said she was worried her father would die in the war or that her mother might not survive her cancer treatment. Should she encourage her to talk, even if it wasn't the most appropriate time? Dinah braced her hands on the edge of her desk and waited.

"Miss Fraser, is Uncle Alex your boyfriend?"

"Hey, Brandon," Alex called out as soon as the door to his spare bedroom opened. Heavy footfalls could be heard in the hall.

The lean teenager appeared with a baseball cap backward over his sandy-brown mop of surfer-dude hair, his perpetual slouch and frown firmly in place. He answered with a grunt, his usual greeting. Alex was probably supposed to feel privileged that he'd responded at all. Whoever thought mood swings were exclusive to teenage girls hadn't met any teenage boys.

"Did you get your homework done?"

Brandon grunted again. Who had kidnapped that sweet little boy he'd known and left this crabby teenager instead? It wasn't a fair trade as far as Alex was concerned.

"Was that a yes?" Alex had considered working out a communication system with the boy—one grunt for *yes* and two for *no*. Maybe they could add eye blinking and finger snapping to increase their vocabulary.

"Yeah," Brandon said.

For the last hour, Alex had lain sprawled on his living

room floor working with Chelsea on an impossible puzzle of Colorado's Pike's Peak. He'd hoped Brandon might join in, too, but he was glad now he hadn't been holding his breath waiting for it. The boy barely paused by the closet for a jacket before heading to the front door.

Alex sat up first and then stood to face the boy. "Where are you going?" He'd hoped to keep the annoyance out of his voice but hadn't quite managed it.

There was only so long that they could all walk around on eggshells, trying not to set off Brandon before Alex had the urge to stomp the shells to dust. Alex figured he'd been plenty patient already, not insisting that Brandon get a haircut and not blowing a gasket over the hat the boy insisted on wearing in the house.

The hot look that appeared in Brandon's deep brown eyes and the tightness of his jaw suggested he didn't think Alex had a right to ask questions, but the boy mumbled an answer anyway. "To Jake's."

"Who is that, where does he live, and what are you going to do there?"

Ah man, when exactly did you turn into your parents? Was it the moment he'd agreed to bring his cousin's two children into his home, or was it a nanosecond after that ill-conceived decision? Either way, he now had everything in common with his parents, except for his dad's pocket protector and his mom's ode-to-the-fifties haircut, and the two were probably laughing down from Heaven right now.

Brandon must have conveniently forgotten the first

two of the three questions because he only answered, "A bunch of us are just going to hang out."

Alex might be new to this parenting business, but did Brandon really think he'd been born the day he accepted guardianship? He'd even survived his teens, somehow, and he knew most of the tricks. "A bunch of us" was probably just code for kids with names like Spike and Rex or, worse yet, Brittney and Nicole. And "hanging out" was something teens did when they didn't have anything better to do than to pack at somebody's house and get into trouble.

He didn't know if real parents had moments of panic where they were certain that a wrong decision could mean disaster for their kids, but Alex understood he was at a crossroads. One wrong move and…oh, he didn't want to think about what could happen.

"I guess I'll see you later then," Brandon said with hope in his voice.

"Nah," Alex said, already shaking his head. "I don't think so." He paused, searching madly for a good reason, and then his gaze landed on the wall clock.

It was already eight o'clock. "I don't think hanging out is a good idea, especially on a school night."

Brandon stared at him as if he'd suddenly grown antlers or something. "Are you kidding?"

Alex shrugged. "Not much of a comedian."

"I live in a prison."

"The food's probably better in a real one," Alex shot back, trying to lighten the tense situation, but Brandon was already out of earshot.

The boy's stomping would have drowned out any

comment he'd made, anyway. Once Brandon reached his room, he rushed in and slammed the door behind him. Soon the house vibrated with the bass sounds of the teen's awful music, but at least he was inside and safe.

Alex released the breath he wasn't aware he'd been holding. He'd dodged a bullet, and he would be foolish to believe it would be the last one Brandon would lob at him. Chelsea wasn't the only one taking her mother's illness hard. Brandon was acting out, and Alex didn't know how to handle him or to help him.

He felt as powerless as he always did when he looked at the ruins of a fire his station had reached too late. Who knew parenting could be so hard? He'd always imagined children as a part of his future, but maybe this was a signal that he wasn't cut out for the job.

The whole nasty scene had taken place with Chelsea lying on the floor and fitting more pieces of the puzzle than Alex had all night. Now the third-grader popped up and moved to sit cross-legged.

"Brandon's mad," she pointed out needlessly.

"I gathered that."

She twirled her fingers through a pile of white pieces destined to find a home somewhere in the puzzle's snow-capped mountains. "He just misses Mom and Dad."

Alex swallowed. He'd been waiting for this, had prepared himself for when she would talk about her feelings, but Chelsea chose to come to him now, when his temporary parenting well was all but bone-dry. Still, he had to step up. He could handle a four-alarm fire, and he could do this.

"You probably miss them, too."

Chelsea's tiny right shoulder lifted and dropped. "I hope they're okay."

"Yeah, me, too, kiddo." He lowered himself to the floor and painfully bent into a pretzel seating position to face her. "I'm sure they will be. God's watching out for them, you know."

"I know. I pray for them at bedtime."

Alex hoped the awe didn't show in his expression. What he wouldn't have given to have that kind of child-like faith. She just listed her petitions to God and waited on Him to do the rest. For Chelsea's sake, Alex hoped she received the answers she wanted because he'd been around long enough to understand now that God sometimes said "no."

"That's good to pray for them." He would have known that she did if he would have remembered to share nighttime prayers with Chelsea, but he could worry about his failures later. This was about her. "It's okay to be scared, too."

"I think Brandon's scared."

Oh, so this was how they were going to play it. A little projection would probably make it easier for her to open up to him. "I'm sure he is."

"He wonders if Dad is afraid at night in the desert. He wants to know if the hospital people remember to put socks on Mom's feet so she doesn't get cold."

A knot formed in Alex's throat so suddenly that he was shocked by the tide of emotion. He cleared his throat to tuck the uncomfortable feelings back under a blanket of proper control. "But Brandon knows that your dad has his friends with him in the desert, right? And he has to know that the doctors and nurses are giving your mom really great care."

She nodded, not looking convinced of either of his assertions. "Brandon probably just needs to spend more time with friends so he can feel better."

Alex's gaze narrowed. He'd assumed that Chelsea was opening up about her feelings. But was this really a sibling attempt to increase Brandon's chances of hanging out? Wow, he'd been played, and he hadn't even realized it.

"Friends, huh?" Frowning, he ruffled her hair. "I'm not letting him—or you for that matter—*hang out* on a school night, and that's all there is to it."

Despite the tough front he was trying to portray, Alex couldn't help blowing out a breath in frustration. "I don't even know this Jake or any of the rest of his friends," he said more to himself than her.

"He should make some friends at church."

Alex opened his mouth to shoot down whatever argument she had next, but he closed it when Chelsea's words sank in. It wasn't a bad idea.

"At church?" He'd reached a new low if he was seeking parenting advice from a nine-year-old, but at least one of them had an idea.

"You know, like a youth group."

"I don't think they have one of those at my church."

"What about at another church?"

Alex thought about it for a few seconds and then frowned. The only local church he knew of that boasted a large, active youth group was Chestnut Grove Community Church, known for its Fall Carnival. That this just happened to be Reverend Fraser's church and where his daughter attended was just a coincidence. It had to be.

"I do know of one at the Chestnut Grove church."

"Let's go there." Chelsea had a strange look in her eyes, but it was probably just enthusiasm.

"Maybe we can visit there sometime soon. Do you think Brandon will go for it?"

"Maybe." Chelsea nodded as if the matter was settled and then flipped back on her belly to return to their puzzle pieces. Immediately she found a pair that fit together and held them up to show him.

"Good job." Alex stretched out next to her on the deep pile carpeting, planting his elbows on the floor and resting his chin in his hands.

He'd done a good job himself tonight, deftly handling Brandon's attitude and managing to get Chelsea to talk to him—all without pulling out a single clump of his own hair. Dinah would be proud of him.

Dinah. He shook his head. Why did she keep turning up in his thoughts these past few days? They barely knew each other. He shouldn't care what Chelsea's teacher thought of his parenting skills, but he would be kidding himself to say he didn't.

As he continued trying to stuff ill-fitting puzzle pieces together, images from earlier in the day flitted through his thoughts. At the school Dinah had looked so pretty with her auburn hair blowing in the wind. He'd been so tempted to tuck one of those soft-looking strands behind her ear that he'd had to put his hands in his pockets to prevent it.

Then and now, he fisted those hands, trying to get a stranglehold on his straying thoughts. He had no business thinking about any woman right now, not when his plate was so full with caring for Karla's children, not when he didn't even know who he was as an individual let alone as part of a couple. Like the pieces of this puzzle, *he* just didn't fit.

Finally back from the journey of his thoughts, Alex glanced over at the section of the puzzle on which Chelsea had been working. She'd already completed the pieces forming one of the tiny mountain peaks.

"I'll have to work harder if I ever want to catch up with you."

Chelsea smiled, but she continued concentrating on her project. With focus like that, no wonder she was such a good student.

After they'd worked together several minutes in silence, Chelsea glanced sidelong at him. "Can I ask you something, Uncle Alex?"

"Sure." He tried not to stiffen too much, imagining questions about enemy fire and terminal illness. Whatever it was, he would answer as honestly as he could.

"Do you have a girlfriend?"

Alex blinked. Okay, he hadn't expected that one. "No. Why do you ask?"

Without bothering to answer his question, she asked one of her own. "Why not?"

He made a dismissive sound in his throat. "No time for that."

"Because of us."

He drew in a startled breath. "Oh, no, kiddo. I didn't mean because of you. I'm just a busy guy." He cleared his throat. Backpedaling was tough work. "It's been great having you here."

She didn't say anything, but he hoped her silence meant she'd forgiven him for his slip. He wasn't blaming her and Brandon for his lack of a social life. He'd made that choice himself.

"You should take Miss Fraser on a date."

Alex started shaking his head the moment the words were out of Chelsea's mouth. "I don't think that's such a good idea."

The only problem was that part of him thought it sounded like a pretty good idea. The part that wasn't rational. The part that took risk for granted every time he donned his gear and climbed aboard the truck to go out on a run.

He needed to ignore that dangerous part as much as he needed to forget about Chelsea's suggestion. As the only adult here, he had to be the sensible one. He didn't know whether he would be able to accomplish any of those things, but the one thing he knew for sure was that he wouldn't be able to get Dinah Fraser out of his mind this evening, either.

Chapter Four

Alex used his forearm to swipe at the sweat on his forehead and started buffing the fire engine's shine again. He didn't care that his hands were already red, and a few blisters had popped out on his palms. By the time he was done with the job this morning, none of the pretty boys at the station would need to primp in the bathroom mirrors because they would be able to see themselves just as well in the truck's shine.

It hadn't been his turn to wax. He'd volunteered, figuring he needed the workout with as many visits to the gym as he'd missed lately. The burn in his biceps convinced him he was right. That the manual labor helped him burn off some stress didn't hurt, either.

Busy trying to expend more energy, he didn't notice anyone approaching until the man tapped him on the shoulder. He jerked around, coming to his feet at the same time.

"Sorry about that, buddy." The dark-headed man,

similar in height and build to Alex, took a step back. He clasped a briefcase in his hands.

Alex frowned. Good thing he'd chosen firefighting instead of police work because he'd probably be lying in a pool of his own blood by now. On the other hand, the guy standing across from him and scanning the perimeter of the room, probably looking for alternate exits, had to be a cop. In his line of work, Alex had been around enough of them to recognize one of the guys in blue when he met one.

"May I help you?"

"Yeah. Are you Alex Donovan?" The man waited for his nod before he continued. "My name is Ross Van Zandt, and I'm a private investigator working with Tiny Blessings Adoption Agency."

Alex swallowed, trying his best not to look surprised. "Good to meet you." Wiping his filthy hand on a towel, he gripped the man's hand.

He would have remembered that name from the newspaper articles even if Ross hadn't made the association to Tiny Blessings. Not that Alex had followed the reports that closely. Or calculated the dates. Or wondered.

Ross patted his briefcase. "I have a private matter I'd like to discuss with you. Is there somewhere we can go to talk?"

The only *private* matter Alex could think of was one he wasn't ready to discuss with anyone, much less allow the rest of the firefighters to overhear, so he glanced around the main bay. A few of the others were working in the office on the other side of the window, and two more had gone to pick up lunch.

Alex cleared his throat and tucked his hands in his jeans pockets. "I guess here is as good as anywhere."

"I'm investigating some falsified birth records from Tiny Blessings, the agency where my wife, Kelly, is the executive director. Have you heard anything about the duplicate birth records?" He lowered his briefcase to the floor at his feet.

"I read about it in the newspaper." Tried to get it out of his mind was a more accurate statement, but both were true.

"Then you know that two sets of doctored documents have been uncovered—the first behind a false wall at the agency office and a second group at the Harcourt mansion." He waited for Alex's nod before he continued. "Are you also aware that you were adopted through the agency during the period in question?"

"Yes, I am." Alex didn't want to say the words, knew that speaking them would open a can of worms, but he did it anyway. "You're here because my records were found with this newest batch, right?"

"That's right," Ross told him.

Alex pulled his hand from his pocket and braced it against the truck, not caring if he marred the shine. He felt numb. Why did having his suspicions confirmed feel like another affront? More lies piling upon earlier lies. No, that wasn't right. These came first, before his parents' lies of omission, though those were the ones that had hurt the most.

"Now you understand that we don't know for sure which, if either, set of birth records is authentic," Ross continued. "But the fact that Barnaby Harcourt built a secret room in his home to hide these makes a strong statement of guilt."

"Sure sounds like it."

Ross stopped and studied him, his gaze narrowing. "Aren't you going to ask me what we've discovered in the records?"

"Why would I?"

"Don't you want to know who your birth parents are? Or at least your birth mother?"

Clearly, the guy didn't get it, so Alex repeated himself. "Why would I want to know? Did you see any requests in my original file to know about my birth parents or even to learn about their medical histories?" He waited for Ross to shake his head before he continued. "Why would I feel any differently about these new files?"

Because Van Zandt probably hadn't even considered that he wouldn't want the information, Alex tried to explain. "You assume that every adopted child is just dying to know who brought him into the world. To know those people who have no more connection to him than sharing a species and some DNA."

Ross tilted his head and studied him, as if considering the idea for the first time. Alex couldn't blame him. Until a year ago, he probably would have thought some of the same things. Now he knew differently, but he realized it wasn't this guy's fault.

"Look…" Alex paused, holding his hands wide. "I really appreciate your making the effort to find me. If I were some guy searching for his birth parents, then all your research would have been a gift."

"You just don't happen to be that guy."

"'Fraid not. But I'm also not your average adoptive child, either."

Ross raised an eyebrow and waited.

"Let's just say I had a rude awakening with that news, but not until after my adoptive parents died."

"You didn't know you were adopted? Oh, sorry, man."

The look of pity in Ross's eyes was the exact reason he hadn't shared that information with many people until now. "Anyway, if I *were* that guy, what were you offering to do for him?"

"I would help him track down a woman who might be his birth mother—the woman whose name is written in a file right in here." Ross glanced at the bag at his feet.

The impulse to reach for that bag took Alex by surprise. He didn't want to know about his biological parents, did he? He'd never wasted any thoughts on those people who didn't care enough about him to keep him.

"You're sure you don't want to know?"

Ross lifted the briefcase that possibly held a piece of the puzzle that had become Alex's life. A puzzle he hadn't asked for. Didn't deserve. But there it was.

"Look, why don't you think about it?" Ross offered. "In the meantime, I have plenty of other files to work through. If you decide you want the answers, just give me the word, and I'll use my resources to help you find them."

"Thanks. I'll think about it." Alex looked up from the briefcase that still tempted him with its information. "I'm sure you could work on some of the other cases for people who'll appreciate your effort a lot more than I would."

"Wouldn't take much for that." Ross chuckled. "Hey, you're one of Eli Cavanaugh's football buddies, aren't you? Have you heard anything about Eli's brother, Ben? He found his birth family not long ago."

"I didn't know, but I'm glad for him, if that's what he wanted."

"It had to be bittersweet for him. Ben found his half siblings, but his biological mother had already passed away."

Ross didn't say more, but his suggestion that Alex shouldn't wait too long hung in the air between them. Would Alex feel even more betrayed if he finally decided to search for his birth mother only to find her name printed on a headstone? Who would answer his questions then?

Ross crossed to the fire engine and walked along its length, admiring it. "You know, there might not be anyone who needs to know the truth more than you do."

"Maybe not."

The topic closed for now, Alex led Ross to the back entrance that faced the parking lot. The two men shook hands once more at the door.

"Thanks again," Alex said. "You know you caught me off guard when you said you were a P.I. The minute I saw you, I thought cop. In my line of work I have to trust my instincts, but lately…"

"Trust those instincts, man. I used to be on the force back in New York."

Alex nodded, sensing that kinship that civil servants share. The private investigator left then, closing the door behind him.

Even after Alex's explanation, it was clear that Ross still didn't understand why he would turn his back on the answers when they were right in front of him. Alex didn't know why he'd even promised to think about letting the P.I. investigate further. Probably just to humor the guy.

Through the window, Alex watched Ross as he headed to his car. Ross waved before he climbed in and closed the door. Alex didn't bother waving back. The other guy probably thought he would eventually get in touch with him, his curiosity growing until he had to know the answers. Alex could tell him right now he wouldn't be calling.

"Who's up for foosball?"

Dinah glanced around the Chestnut Grove Youth Center for any takers, but no one could hear her over the chatter and laughter in the room. Tyler and Dylan just continued capturing enemies in their board game, Tiffany and Gina sat mesmerized by the animated movie they probably knew by heart and Jeremy and Billy wrestled on the couch.

With all the chaos, Dinah didn't hear her mother's approach until Naomi Fraser touched her on the arm, startling her.

"Here, try this." The redhead pressed a child's-style, wireless microphone into her daughter's hand, mischief shining in her vivid blue eyes. "I would give you a whistle, but the power might be too much for you."

"Gee, thanks, Mom." But her frown softened. Flipping on the switch, she tapped her hand a few times on the microphone's head, sending out a crackly, pounding sound. To her surprise, the room fell silent.

She covered the mike with her hand. "Wow, Dad sure has this group trained."

"Haven't you noticed that when your father uses the microphone, he's usually saying grace before he hands out snacks?" Naomi winked.

"I can't believe you set me up. Now everyone's going to be hounding me for food."

Naomi rolled her eyes as she brushed her hand back through her no-nonsense short hair. "Just make your announcement before they go back to what they were doing."

"Fine." She turned back to her audience and uncovered the mike. "Hey, everybody. Our foosball tournament starts in ten minutes. Do we have any other late entries so we can make teams?"

She scanned the group for any takers.

Near the front entrance a boy with light brown hair stood with his arms crossed. Not a likely joiner. She couldn't get a real good look at the boy because he had hair falling over his eyes, but he still looked familiar.

She knew why he did the second Alex and Chelsea came through the door. Though both the boy's hair and eye color were a few shades darker, his square jaw and distinctive, straight nose were too similar to Chelsea's for him not to be her brother, Brandon. If the two children bore any resemblance to Alex, she didn't see it yet.

Chatter erupted again as the teens noticed the visitors in their midst. Soon the three of them were surrounded by a bunch of youths giving them the welcome treatment. Somehow Alex extricated himself from the crowd and made his way over to Dinah.

"Friendly bunch, aren't they?"

"We try to be." Her throat felt dry. She cleared it, covering her mouth with her fist. "What are you doing here?" Was it because she would be there? No, that was ridiculous. He couldn't possibly have known that she volunteered at the center that her father also ran. But he did know her dad was pastor of this church, so…

"Sorry. I thought the youth center was open to anybody. Youth, I mean. But if it's not…" He let his words trail away, waiting for her to explain.

Again she struggled with the frog taking up long-term residence in her throat. "It is. Of course. I just meant—" Stopping herself because she didn't know what she'd meant, she lowered her gaze to the floor. That was when she noticed the microphone still dangling from her free hand. She didn't have to examine it closer to remember that she hadn't switched it off yet.

Apparently, she was the only one who hadn't noticed until then that she was broadcasting their brief conversation, and now more than a few confused faces were trained on her, their owners wondering why she was trying to uninvite their guests. Her mother lifted an eyebrow and smiled. Naomi Fraser never missed much.

Dinah tapped the microphone again. "Let's try this again. The tournament is about to begin. Anyone can play as long as you sign up in the next five minutes. Now would anyone like to introduce our guests?"

Tiffany raised her hand to do the honors, and Dinah couldn't help but smile. The slightly plump teen, who was a bit of a tomboy, had carried a torch for Billy for a long time, but he might have some competition in Brandon.

"I'd like you all to meet Brandon and Chelsea White and their, uh, guardian…" Tiffany shot a questioning look at the new kids.

"Alex Donovan," Dinah said, filling in the blank too quickly. Alex was kind enough to look away instead of picking this moment to trap her in one of his infamous stares.

"Anybody else want to play?" Dinah asked. "If so, I need you to sign up immediately at the tennis table."

Not surprising given that the center had guests, there was a renewed interest in foosball, and she registered five more participants, Brandon included, before the competition began. Only after the start of the first game could Dinah make her way back to her mother, who just happened to be talking to Alex.

"…were looking for a youth group for the kids, and my own church doesn't have one," Alex was saying when she reached them.

Of course he'd come here because of the children. Why else would someone visit a youth center other than to find Christian fellowship for young people? When was she going to stop wishing Alex's words or motives had something to do with her instead of with the children in his care? Just because Chelsea thought Alex was Dinah's boyfriend didn't mean he was interested in her—or even that he should be.

"Oh, Dinah, Alex says you two know each other." Naomi didn't say more, didn't need to. Those mischievous eyes spoke volumes.

"We had a conference about Chelsea at school."

"And a false alarm from what Chelsea tells me."

Dinah glanced at her mother, who could barely contain her amusement, and then looked around for Chelsea. The child had joined the teens in the movie-viewing area but was watching the three adults out of the corner of her eye.

"That, too." Dinah supposed she should be grateful the child had mentioned only the fire alarm and hadn't embarrassed Alex in front of her mother by bringing up her boyfriend/girlfriend questions.

"Alex has been guardian for his cousin's children while she's undergoing cancer treatment. He's helping them work through the tough times."

"Looks like he's doing a great job." Naomi pointed to the foosball table where Brandon had just scored a goal and was high-fiving Jeremy.

Alex stared at Brandon, surprise written all over his face. "He hasn't smiled like that in months," he explained when he caught the two women watching him.

"Then look how smart you were for bringing Brandon here."

"Forcing is more like it," Alex said.

Dinah grinned. "Whatever it takes, I guess."

"Chelsea looks like she's having fun, too." Naomi indicated with a tilt of her head the TV-viewing area where several of the younger girls had squeezed in with Chelsea on the couch.

Alex didn't say anything, but he did appear pleased with himself. His grin was contagious. Whether he'd come for her sake or not, Dinah was happier than she ought to have been that he was there.

"Well…"

Dinah turned her head and found her mother waiting—not for too long, she hoped.

Naomi just grinned and adjusted her pearls. "I'd better round up that husband of mine and see what he has planned for snacks today. This crowd's going to be hungry once we have a foosball champion."

As Naomi moved past them, she turned back and gave a wink that only Dinah could see.

"Your mom's nice," Alex said as she moved away.

"Yeah, she's just a peach."

"Peach?" He lifted an eyebrow. "She's as sweet as the whole pie from what I can see."

Her gaze flicked to Naomi's retreating form, and she forgot her sarcasm. "She's that, too."

Would she and Alex continue standing there, extolling her mother's virtues. She searched around for something clever to say, something that would make him laugh, but she had nothing.

"Hey, this place is great."

Alex took his time looking around at the game area, the TV spot and the group of tables where they usually doled out pizza. He wasn't waiting for her to fill the silence at all. Why was she trying so hard to impress him when he didn't seem to expect it? She'd been exposed to members of the opposite gender many times, even dated some, so why did Alex Donovan make her feel like a seventh-grader with her first crush? No, not a crush. She didn't *do* crushes. But something.

"You guys have to be proud of yourselves, putting together a place like this," he said, trying again.

"It was my dad's project in the beginning. He thought it was a great way to reach young people."

"The reverend has to be a busy man with running the church and this center. I don't know how he finds time for everything he does."

With a slight tilt of his head, Alex indicated Reverend Fraser, who'd just come through the kitchen door, using both hands to balance pizza boxes above his head. His wire-rim glasses were sliding down his nose, and his silver hair stuck out in tufts, but he had no free hands to right his appearance.

Alex must have read the question in her eyes because he explained, "I worked with your dad on the holiday toy drive last Christmas. This church's drop-off site was one of the most successful."

"So that's how you knew him."

"And that's why your name sounded so familiar to me. Why didn't you say who your parents were when I asked?"

The feeling that struck Dinah reminded her of being called to the board to do a problem in algebra when the FOIL Method was about as clear as swamp water. Part of her explanation here made sense, but the other part was muddier than she liked.

"Some people have a strange reaction when they discover I'm a PK—preacher's kid—so I usually don't throw it out there right away."

Alex moved his head back and forth as if considering and then nodded. He either accepted what she'd said, or he decided not to press. Either way, she was grateful.

"I saw that this place is open every afternoon after school and most of the day on Saturdays. Does the Fraser family single-handedly keep the place running?"

She shook her head at that impossible notion. "Mom and I work here regularly, as does Scott Crosby, the assistant pastor, and Caleb Williams, the youth minister. Even my younger sister, Ruth, helps when she's home from college. But without all the other volunteers from church, we couldn't keep the doors here open."

She waited for him to scan the room again and see the massive scale of the project before she continued. "I volunteer here most Tuesdays and Thursdays after school."

As soon as she'd spoken the words, she clamped her mouth shut. *Way to go, Dinah.* Could she be any more obvious that she wanted him to know where *she* was on Tuesday and Thursday afternoons, just in case he wondered?

If he picked up on her flub, he didn't let it show. "All the volunteers should be commended." His gaze lingered on her face, warming her and making it clear which volunteer he expected to accept that compliment.

"The center has been a hit with the kids. Yours included."

His eyes widened, showing he still wasn't accustomed to anyone referring to his young charges as his. Maybe it was temporary, but they were definitely his responsibility. Alex looked over in time to see Brandon throw his hands into the air and do some sort of victory dance over a goal.

Alex nodded as if coming to a conclusion. "This place is going to be good for the kids. Brandon especially. He needs a chance to spend time with other Christian kids."

"Then you'll be back?"

"I think so."

"I'm—I mean, *we're*—glad."

A whoop went up from the crowd then, signaling that one of the girls had scored this time, and Alex turned toward the commotion, but a small smile remained on his lips.

Chelsea slipped between them then and slid an arm through Alex's. "You see, Uncle Alex. This place is fun."

Alex turned around and hoisted the child up on his hip as if she were three instead of nine, but Chelsea didn't seem to mind. "It is fun. You were right. Do you think we should come back?"

The child leaned her forehead into Alex's until they could exchange butterfly kisses with their eyelashes. "Every day."

"How about a few times a week? That sounds like a better idea, don't you think?"

Chelsea's disappointment showed, and she stared into his eyes for several seconds, as if trying to decide whether theatrics would help her get her way. Dinah hoped he didn't cave in to the demands because it would set a precedent that wouldn't help him later.

She'd seen plenty of experienced parents make that mistake.

But Chelsea only shrugged and lifted her head away. "Okay. But the youth center is having this fall carnival with rides and everything, and there's a lot of stuff that needs to be done to get ready for it. Stuff beginning tomorrow. Every day."

Alex started shaking his head as he lowered the miniature manipulator to the ground. "I don't know—"

"But, Uncle Alex, it will be so much fun. The big girls said we could help. They need grown-ups to help, too."

He turned back to Dinah, a plea for assistance so plain in his eyes that she couldn't help grinning.

"Well, Chelsea's right. The annual carnival is October twentieth. It's usually the second week of October, but the Main Street repaving project won't be completed until the fifteenth, and we'll need all the side-street parking that's available since—" She stopped herself, figuring he didn't need all the gory details.

"Anyway, the carnival is coming up, and it's going to be bigger than ever this year," she said. "We're adding rides in the church parking lot as well as all the regular booths outside and in the gym."

"So what you're saying is you need all the help you can get," he finished for her.

Dinah shrugged, signaling with a brush of her hand for Chelsea to skedaddle off to her newfound friends so the grown-ups could talk. She could give him an easy out, but the idea of seeing Alex Donovan regularly for several days did hold a certain appeal. The event would benefit the center, and that was the important thing.

"We do need more volunteers—teens and adults—to do preparations for the fall carnival." She shot him a sidelong glance, only to find that Alex's frown was focused on her now.

She rushed to explain. "You know, doing things like assembling equipment for the carnival games. We wouldn't expect anybody here to put the Tilt-A-Whirl together or anything." She paused, glancing at him again. "We're using trained professionals for that."

"Good. I'd hate knowing I assembled a ride that created human catapults."

"If you can do that, remind me not to let you handle any power tools."

"Not even a power screwdriver to assemble the balloon-dart booth?" He was grinning again now.

"Then you're in?"

"How can I not be with you and Chelsea teaming up against me?"

Caleb Williams chose that moment to approach them. "Hey, Dinah, I hear you've recruited some new talent for the carnival."

"Alex Donovan," Dinah said before turning to the black-haired man, "I'd like you to meet Caleb Williams, our amazing youth minister."

"I don't know about the amazing part, but it's good to meet you." Caleb pumped his hand. "Thanks for volunteering. We sure can use the extra help this year since we're ramping up the carnival and everything."

"It does sound like a big job."

Caleb's confident smile suggested he was up to the challenge. "Well, we had to do something amazing if we wanted to outdo last year's carnival. Last time the kids made all the adults dress in costumes, so they'd remember what it was like to play. This year we want the kids to be just as wowed as we were. I think it will be a blast for all of us."

When the youth minister excused himself and headed over to the video area, Alex turned back to Dinah. "Okay, I'm giving in for the sake of the carnival. Brandon, Chelsea and I will put in as many hours as we can in the next week or so."

Alex paused, crossing his arms. "But I'm telling you right now, after the carnival is over, the kids will only be coming here a few times a week, just like I said."

Dinah grinned, understanding how important it would be to him to establish his authority by not going back on his earlier decision. "Way to stick to your guns, Mr. Guardian."

Alex turned his forefingers and thumbs into a pair of imaginary pistols and tucked them into an equally pretend holster at his hips.

Dinah was still enjoying his acting when something he'd said earlier came to mind. "Wait. Didn't I hear you tell Chelsea she was right? Was it her idea to come here?"

After a quick peek to where his young cousin was now holding court among the older girls, he turned back to Dinah and shrugged. "It is pitiful, I guess, taking parenting tips from a third-grader."

"Not pitiful." But she couldn't keep a straight face.

"I know it is, but in my defense, my nine-year-old counselor did have a good idea. Chelsea suggested that we find a youth group so Brandon could make some new friends."

"And you said you didn't have one at your church?" She knew it was a sneaky way of trying to ascertain whether Alex attended church or not, but she couldn't help herself. If he didn't already have a church home, she had one she could recommend—just for the sake of outreach, of course.

"No, my church is too small for that. I never needed a youth group before, anyway."

"You have a point there." That she was at once pleased and disappointed that Alex attended church somewhere else shamed her. She couldn't claim an interest in only his spiritual health when her feelings were so conflicted.

"Anyway, part of this grand scheme was all my idea." He didn't hide how pleased he was about that. "Chelsea didn't know about this youth center, but I did. I'd read about all the activities here in the newspaper even before I met your dad. Every once in a while I get things right."

Dinah chewed the side of her lower lip as her gaze flitted from scene to scene in the room without really landing on any one of them. With Alex feeling confident about one of his parenting decisions, it didn't seem right for her to rain all over his parade.

It just wouldn't be the Christian thing to do. Maybe God wouldn't mind this time if she let Alex continue believing something that made him happy.

When she turned back to Alex again, he was studying her. "Okay, what are you not telling me?"

She pressed her lips together for a few seconds and then spoke. "In class the other day, I told my students about this youth center where I volunteered."

"You mean she knew about this place all along?"

"Afraid so. She must have thought the center sounded like fun." She expected his expression to fall just as his confidence must have, but after taking a few seconds to digest the information, Alex grinned.

"Then I'd better watch out with this little one. If she decides she wants a sports car, there'll be a Lamborghini in the drive by the weekend."

They both laughed at that, though Dinah's laughter was more of the nervous variety. What if Chelsea had developed some ridiculous notion that her teacher and her guardian should be together? That was silly. The little girl probably just wanted to try out the youth center. Still, Dinah had the odd feeling she should thank Chelsea for bringing them all together tonight.

Chapter Five

Chelsea climbed off her school bus and hurried into the building behind several other children, all of them carrying near-matching backpacks except for the key chains and toys that dangled from the zippers. No one was moving fast enough this morning, in her opinion.

She hadn't been this excited to go to school since last spring when her mom used to kiss her on the cheek and pat her on top of the head every morning before she got on the bus. *Since before Mom got sick.* The thought tried to make her sad as so many of her thoughts had lately, but Chelsea made herself think about all the happy things at the youth center until her eyes quit burning.

Last night had been so much fun, even if she hadn't won any games in air hockey and even if they'd had to go home just before the end of *Dumbo.* The big girls had let her play with them, and Nikki, who was sixteen, had even let Chelsea comb her long blond hair. Someday Chelsea planned to have hair just as long and pretty as Nikki's.

Brandon had liked the youth center, too, whether he would say so or not. He'd smiled a lot and laughed sometimes, and he hadn't called Chelsea a name even once all night.

The best part of the youth center, though, had been seeing Uncle Alex and Miss Fraser together, but Chelsea didn't think she should tell them that. Uncle Alex had said it wouldn't be a good idea to ask Miss Fraser on a date, but he liked her. Even Chelsea could see that, and she was only in third grade. So why couldn't Miss Fraser see it?

Grown-ups. Would she ever understand them?

But that didn't matter today. Her idea was just the best. Everyone would think so later.

"Chelsea, please slow down in the halls," the principal called from behind her.

Turning her head, she spoke over her shoulder. "Sorry, Mrs. Pratt."

She tried to make her feet move slower even though she wanted to skip. Once she reached her classroom, she hung her jacket on the hook with her name next to it and placed her backpack in her cubby before taking a seat at her desk.

Miss Fraser looked so pretty this morning. Her light blue blouse and its matching tank top made her eyes look so blue. She wore her pretty red hair in a ponytail today though Chelsea wished she'd worn it down the way she did sometimes.

"Good morning, class," Miss Fraser said as she stepped to the front.

"Good morning, Miss Fraser," Chelsea chorused with her classmates.

"Everyone please rise for the Pledge of Allegiance."

Chelsea recited the words as loudly as she could, her hand perched right over her heart. It was the same routine they followed each morning. Next would be attendance and the lunch count. It was strange: even the regular stuff felt more exciting this morning.

Today would be even more fun than the youth center. All she had to do was wait through math, social studies and gym, and the time would be here.

She could hardly wait.

Dinah startled at a sound that was becoming as familiar as that cranky bleep of her alarm clock in the morning. Not again. Maybe it was just a momentary electrical lapse, and all would return to the normal low rumble that signaled education was taking place here.

But as hard as she wished for it to stop, the fire alarm continued to blare. This was a frustrating way to end the school week. She'd hoped that last time would be *the* last time, but at this point it seemed unlikely.

"Everyone, please grab your jackets and line up at the door." At least this time they wouldn't freeze while they stood there at the curb, waiting for the all-clear signal. "I need you to be quiet until we reach the flagpole."

"Is it another false alarm, Miss Fraser?" Lily Polson called out.

Dinah pulled her own coat from her storage cabinet and put her index finger to her lips in a call for silence. "I don't know that. We always have to take a fire alarm seriously."

She remembered the exact person who'd told her

that, the same person who would be disappointed in the students here if this was another false alarm.

"How many fire trucks do you think will come this time?" Kellan Stolz exclaimed as they started down the hall.

Dinah spun to face her students and then pinned him in her stare. "Kellan, I need you to be quiet."

He straightened up after that, and somehow they made it out of the building. As the wind pelted her face, Dinah shivered despite her jacket. Already, she could hear the sirens of the approaching fire engines.

Once she reached the flagpole, Dinah pulled out her grade book and started checking off the names on the list. The first half of the alphabet went well, but when she reached the bottom end of the second half, something gripped inside her.

Where was Chelsea?

Her pulse thudding in her chest, Dinah scanned her line of students again and then a few of the lines next to them. She couldn't panic; at least, she couldn't let the children see. They were counting on her to keep them safe and calm.

Continuing her scan as inconspicuously as possible, Dinah racked her brain to remember when she'd seen Chelsea last. Had it been while they were gathering their coats and lining up at the door? But as hard as she tried, she couldn't picture Chelsea next to their coat hooks and cubbies.

Two fire engines and two smaller trucks pulled into the lot, and just like last time, two firefighters hurried into the building.

That was when Dinah remembered. Of course. Chelsea hadn't been at her classroom door because she'd taken the restroom pass just before the alarm sounded.

Did that mean Chelsea was still inside? What if this wasn't a false alarm at all? Panic clogged Dinah's throat, and as hard as she fought against it, she wasn't winning.

Dear God, please be with Chelsea, she prayed, but Dinah needed to be with her, too.

Stepping over to the next line of students, Dinah leaned close to Lydia Shultz, the second-grade teacher who'd been at Grove Elementary since Dinah was a student there herself.

"Will you watch my class for a few minutes?" Her whisper sounded desperate, even to her own ears. "I need to get inside."

"You know you can't go back in, Dinah. Not until the bell. We don't even know if it's a false alarm."

"I have to go. One of my students is in there."

She rushed across the blacktop only to stop where she stood when the front door of the building swung wide. Principal Alyce Pratt emerged, holding Chelsea's hand. The child looked fine, even if she wasn't wearing her jacket. Rather than rattled, as Dinah expected she would be, Chelsea appeared strangely calm.

At least she was okay. *Thank you, Father.* Dinah slowly released the breath she'd been holding. She wanted to run to the little girl and to see for herself that she was okay, but before she could do it, the door opened again. With his helmet under his arm, Alex tromped out with another firefighter. His posture was stiff, and he had fury stamped all over his face.

Realization dawned like the opening scene of a bad dream. Chelsea had pulled the fire alarm? No, it didn't seem possible. Not sweet little Chelsea whom Dinah had known for more than a year. Chelsea who was nice to everyone and insisted on trapping spiders in the classroom to release them outside.

But as the principal approached her, with Alex as close behind them as he could be without stepping on their heels with his heavy boots, Dinah knew it was the truth. That same child had placed all of her schoolmates and teachers at risk for a silly thrill. Did Chelsea think it was worth it now that she'd been caught and would have to face the consequences of her actions?

Taking a few steps closer, she stared down at the young lawbreaker. "Chelsea?"

Dinah wished she could hide the disappointment in her voice, but she couldn't. She expected the child's shoulders to droop and for those light brown eyes to be filled with guilt as they looked back at her.

Chelsea showed neither of those things. Instead, a small, confusing smile appeared on her face. Dinah turned a questioning glance toward Alex, but his grim expression didn't spare any answers. The bell rang before she had the chance to ask for them.

"Why don't the four of us go in my office for a little chat?" Mrs. Pratt suggested.

Dinah swallowed, her insides clamping tight. In her three years of teaching, she'd had to face students with their parents a few times. She'd even been present for discussions that involved the principal when the necessity arose. So why did this time feel so different?

She tried to reconcile it while she crossed to her students, making arrangements for the third-grade paraprofessional to cover her class for a few minutes. She was still the teacher here, and Chelsea was still her student. Alex and Mrs. Pratt were each present in their roles, though Alex did play a dual role of civil servant and guardian.

Still, there was no argument that the situation felt different. It was irrational; she understood that. But as they passed through the school doors and entered the office to the left, Dinah had this odd feeling that she would sit on both sides of the desk this time. She would help to dole out proper discipline as an educator, but at the same time she would share Alex's embarrassment and self-blame as he faced this difficult time with the child he loved.

Alex took one of the seats the diminutive principal offered in an office that was already crowded before she'd stuffed the four of them in it and closed the door. It was stifling. He released the remaining fasteners on his coat and settled into the padded chair. He didn't even want to look at the child seated next to him, though he figured he didn't have any choice.

He could only imagine the ribbing he would take later at the station. *Some guardian you are, Donovan. What will you teach next at your house, arson techniques?*

"It's been an eventful morning," Mrs. Pratt said as she rested her elbows on the desk.

For several long seconds, the principal focused on Chelsea, who sat without squirming. Dinah, on the other hand, kept shifting in her seat and wringing her hands, as if she were the one in trouble instead of the girl. Finally, Mrs. Pratt glanced to her right and left to draw the two adults into the conversation.

"We all have an idea why we're here, but to bring everyone up to speed, our custodian, Mr. Vinton, witnessed Chelsea pulling the fire alarm this morning in the grade three-four hallway." She turned back to Alex, a sad smile on her lips. "I would have had to call Mr. Donovan in for a meeting this morning, but since he was already here…"

Letting her words fall away, the principal turned back to Chelsea. "Now, young lady, I have a few questions for you. First, did you pull the fire alarm any of the other times, or is this the first time?"

"Just this time."

It had to be the smile on Chelsea's face that made Alex's hands grip the armrests of his chair tighter. How could she not be sorry?

The principal nodded, no judgment in her expression. "You've never been in trouble before. Why did you choose to change that today by pulling the alarm? Did you understand that making a false alarm is breaking the law?"

Chelsea stiffened and drew her eyebrows together. "Am I going to jail?"

Appearing surprised by the child's answer, Mrs. Pratt cleared her throat. "No…not yet, anyway."

The threat didn't have teeth, and Alex knew it, but

he didn't contradict the educator. Even if it was illegal to create a false alarm by tripping the lever at a pull station, nobody at the Chestnut Grove Police Department would be willing to haul a nine-year-old off to jail for what could only amount to a practical joke.

"But you knew it was wrong, didn't you, Chelsea?" Alex couldn't help prodding. She didn't seem to feel guilty, and he couldn't relax until Chelsea experienced at least a little remorse for what she'd done. He could just imagine the miniature delinquent he would be giving back to Karla when she was released from the hospital. "We talked about that after the last false alarm here. Don't you remember?"

"I remember," she said in a small voice.

"Then answer Mrs. Pratt's question. Why did you do it?"

Chelsea gave him one of those strange kid looks that he was beginning to recognize, the one that said, "Don't you get it, you clueless adult?" It was one of Brandon's favorite expressions, so Alex knew it well. Instead of answering, Chelsea glanced at Dinah and then looked back at him. Was it hope that he saw dancing in her eyes?

Alex swallowed, a disturbing suspicion settling in his gut. No, Chelsea was too smart to do something like that. At least he hoped she was.

"Because you would come," Chelsea said finally.

He groaned inside as she confirmed his suspicion.

Dinah, who'd been quiet until now, straightened in her seat. "Of course he would come, Chelsea. Firefighters have to take alarms seriously even if you—"

She stopped suddenly and turned from the child she'd been addressing to him. From her crimson cheeks and her wide eyes, he could guess that the realization had dawned as disturbingly on her as it had on him. She chewed her bottom lip, and her gaze darted away from him.

Silence enclosed the four of them until the principal cleared her throat to fracture the quiet. "What am I missing here, Miss Fraser?"

Instead of waiting for Dinah to find her words, Alex forced himself to begin. "This all appears to be a misunderstanding."

"Mr. Donovan, I already explained that our custodian caught Chelsea in the act of pulling the alarm."

He shook his head, a nervous chuckle bubbling in his throat. "No, I'm not questioning your employee's word. I have no doubt that she set off the alarm. I'm just saying that it was a misunderstanding that inspired our little incident here."

Mrs. Pratt leaned back and crossed her arms, taking on a tough stance that no doubt served her well in her chosen profession. "I'm afraid you're going to have to explain."

Gripping her hands together, Dinah leaned forward and opened her mouth to speak, but Alex shook his head.

"If you don't mind, Miss Fraser, I'd like to handle this one."

But instead of turning back to the principal and giving what could only be an uncomfortable explanation for all involved, he turned in his chair to face Chelsea.

"Sweetheart, did you pull the alarm because you wanted to bring Miss Fraser and me together in the same building?"

"Sure, Uncle Alex."

That she didn't even bother to hesitate or to deny it struck him as gutsy, but he couldn't allow himself to be proud of her for these antics. Besides, he couldn't be proud of any action that humiliated Dinah Fraser as much as Chelsea's had.

Mrs. Pratt started to say something else, but he held her off by continuing his questioning. "Why did you want to do that?"

Again, Chelsea gave him one of those dumb-parent looks, but she answered anyway. "If you were here together, then you could ask her out on a date."

He'd been giving the child his full attention, but when he caught sight of the principal again, she was pressing her lips together in a firm line, as if trying not to smile. He couldn't blame her.

If this were happening to someone else, he would have been rolling on the floor, only to feel guilty for his insensitivity later. As it stood, he was one of the unfortunate targets of this matchmaking scheme, and he could only try to survive with some small part of his dignity intact.

"Now, Chelsea, we've already discussed this."

Chelsea nodded. Okay, that wasn't the best beginning he could have chosen. Now the two women had to wonder why Chelsea and he had discussed this matter and what conclusions they'd drawn, but he wasn't about to go into that right now. He cleared his throat and tried again.

"I know that you love your teacher. Miss Fraser has been great to you." He couldn't help flicking a look Dinah's way, but she was staring at her clenched hands. "Also, I know that you have these ideas about the two of us dating, but our social lives are not your business."

Even with that comment, Chelsea's smile remained unchanged. She appeared pleased with herself that her plan had been successful. She'd brought Dinah and him together, all right. Together in embarrassment. Somehow, he had to make her understand that.

"What you've done today was wrong."

As soon as he said it, Chelsea's shoulders curled forward and her expression fell. Strange how he longed to draw the words back into his mouth and coax her smile to return when he understood that she needed to be disciplined for her actions. So this was what parents meant when they said, "This hurts me a lot more than it hurts you."

Dinah lifted a hand to interrupt him, but he shook his head again. He was Chelsea's guardian, and in her parents' absence, his responsibility was to help her learn to make good choices.

"You put your teachers and classmates in danger when you pulled that alarm. You, and the other students who set off the pull stations, have taught your friends not to take a fire alarm seriously." He shook his head to emphasize the grave point. "Someone who doesn't take an alarm seriously could get hurt." *Or killed,* he almost said.

"And if there were a real fire somewhere else, the department wouldn't have any trucks or firefighters to send to it." Alex stopped himself when Chelsea's lip trembled. He couldn't tell if he'd taken his point too far or just far enough, but he knew he'd reached her.

"I'm…sorry…Uncle Alex," she managed to get out as two huge tears trailed down her face.

Slipping one arm around her shoulders, Alex used the other hand to wipe the tears from her cheeks. "I know you are, punky. I know you weren't trying to hurt anybody when you pulled that alarm. It probably seemed like a really clever idea."

The smile was back, though a weak one, combined with a case of the sniffles.

"Clever idea or not," Dinah began in a kind tone, "we can't have students pulling fire alarms in our school. It's just too dangerous."

Alex nodded, ready to let the others participate in the discussion. "Miss Fraser's right, Chelsea. There's going to be consequences for your actions—here at school and at home."

At that, Mrs. Pratt pushed up her wire-frame glasses and took charge of the meeting. "At school, young lady, that is going to mean working with the custodian, emptying trash cans and cleaning the dry-erase boards. You'll need to stay for an extra thirty minutes each afternoon for two weeks. You'll also be expected to spend your recesses in the office for those two weeks."

"Lunch recess, too?" Chelsea looked as though someone had stolen her dog.

"I'm afraid so."

Alex was nodding his agreement with the punishment when Chelsea turned from the principal back to him.

"At home?" Chelsea asked.

With a flourish of her hand, Mrs. Pratt turned the meeting over to Alex.

The wheels started spinning in his thoughts, but nothing came to mind. He'd never handed out punishments before and had no idea what worked with a nine-year-old.

Dinah glanced over at him and grinned. "A lot of my parents take away special privileges as a consequence. Chelsea, do you remember which privileges Brandon lost last year when he got in trouble for making prank calls?"

Alex glanced sidelong at Dinah, and nodded his thanks. Of course Dinah knew about the time that Brandon got into trouble. Teachers tended to be privy to all kinds of private information from their students' homes.

He turned back to Chelsea, trying not to wonder what the child had told her teacher about him. "Do you remember?"

"Mom said he couldn't talk on the telephone, and he couldn't have playdates," Chelsea said.

"Playdates, huh?" He doubted Brandon would appreciate a term like that. Still, he was grateful for the information.

Maybe he was new at it, but he could do this. He just needed to decide which of her privileges were more important to her and to limit them for now.

"You won't be able to have playdates, either, until your punishment at school is finished. And you can't watch any TV," he continued. "I want you to understand how serious this thing today was."

"Am I grounded?" Chelsea asked, tears back in her eyes.

Alex shook his head, drawing his eyebrows together. "I didn't say—"

"If I'm grounded, we can't go work on the stuff for the fall carnival."

So that was it. Now he knew which of her privileges was most important to her. Alex thought for a moment before speaking.

"I didn't say anything about grounding you, though maybe I should have. But no, the people in the youth group need our help for the carnival, and we've already volunteered. It wouldn't be fair to punish all of them or Brandon for your behavior." The thought crossed his mind that the plan would have punished him, too, but he chose to ignore it.

Chelsea nodded, her tears disappearing as quickly as they'd appeared.

Dinah clapped her hands once. "Now that that's settled, Chelsea, why don't you go back to class? The adults need to talk for a few minutes. I'll be there shortly."

"Yeah, go ahead." Alex put his arm around the child and squeezed and then helped her to stand.

As soon as Chelsea had left the room and closed the door behind her, Dinah turned back to her principal. "I am so sorry about this, Mrs. P. I had no idea…" Her words trailed off as a grin spread across the principal's face.

"Well, I've been in education a long time, and I thought I'd seen everything." Mrs. Pratt shook her head, still smiling.

"Leave it to my family to prove you wrong," Alex said.

Laughing for a few seconds, they all stopped at about the same time, as if they jointly recognized it was time to deal with the serious matter at hand.

"Something has to be done about all of these false alarms, though," Alex said, verbalizing what they all knew to be true. "You could go to the trouble of installing glass enclosures around pull stations so the glass has to be broken before an alarm can be set."

Slipping off her glasses, Mrs. Pratt closed her eyes and pinched the bridge of her nose between her thumb and forefinger. With school budgets always being tight, she probably was considering that expense in terms of the bottom line.

"But since this is a place of learning," Alex continued, "I thought you might want to consider an educational alternative."

The principal's eyes opened at that, and she put her glasses back on. Dinah shifted, looking interested, as well.

"What would you two think if I volunteered to give fire safety presentations in the school?"

"I'd say you're hired," Mrs. Pratt deadpanned.

Despite the easy sale he'd made, he continued his presentation. "Now before you turn me down, hear me out. This will be about your students' safety, in and out of school. There have been too many pulled alarms this year, so I want the kids to understand about the complacency that comes with crying wolf."

Dinah leaned her head forward so he noticed her. "Are you finished? May we speak now?"

He sat back and crossed his arms. "Sure."

The principal squeezed her eyes closed as if considering before opening them again. "You drive a hard bargain, Mr. Donovan, so I guess we'll have to take you up on it."

"It will be great for the kids," Dinah chimed. "They think firefighters are real heroes."

"And you don't?" he asked.

Dinah didn't answer, but her cheeks reddened in that attractive way they always did.

"You've got to give Chelsea credit for her inventiveness in pulling the fire alarm," Mrs. Pratt said, drawing their attention back to her.

Alex stared at her. "You're not proud of her, are you?"

"Of course not. And don't you tell her what I said, either." She waved an index finger at them. "But I have to say, I've never seen a matchmaker go to that kind of length to bring two people together."

"Leave it to Chelsea for reaching to new heights in the amateur matchmaking business," Alex said.

Dinah chuckled with him. "She's an overachiever, all right."

Both of them looked to Mrs. Pratt, expecting her to chime in, as well. Instead, she settled her elbows on her desk and rested her chin in the cradle formed by her hands. Silence only made the tiny office feel smaller and made Alex's clothes feel warmer. Sweat trickled from his temple, and he brushed it away with the back of his hand.

"Do you have something to say?" Alex asked when he couldn't stand any more.

The educator removed her glasses in the practiced move of one used to being thought of as wise. "Have you ever considered that Chelsea might be right?"

Chapter Six

The first time they'd visited the Chestnut Grove Youth Center, Alex had figured that the place couldn't be any more chaotic, but as he looked around that Tuesday evening, he knew he'd been wrong.

Around him, teens and grown-ups alike milled about carrying two-by-fours, lettered signs and buckets of paint and brushes to different "centers" where work was under way on everything from the ring-toss and pie-eating booths to the ever popular Pick-A-Duck booth.

Alex was tempted to back out of the door he'd come through. He and the children didn't really know these people. This wasn't even his church. Anyway, the folks here appeared to have whatever they were doing under control. Brandon and Chelsea stood next to him, taking in the same scene, but instead of appearing reluctant to get started, both of them looked as if they couldn't wait to get their hands dirty.

"Alex Donovan, is that you?"

Alex recognized the tall man with dirty-blond hair immediately. "Hey, Eli."

His old friend crossed the room in long strides and hugged him, patting him several times on the back. "How have you been? I've barely seen you since you moved to Chestnut Grove, but I'd heard you've been busy." Eli glanced at Alex's young cousins.

"Brandon and Chelsea, this is Dr. Cavanaugh."

"Hi, guys."

The children greeted Eli politely and then disappeared into the crowd, making the decision for Alex that they wouldn't be leaving.

Across the room, one of the older boys narrowly missed another boy's head as he passed with a sign. "This place is a madhouse," Alex said.

"It does get crazy this time of year, but the carnival is great." Eli had been watching a group of teens painting a mouth-shaped sign for the beanbag toss, but then he turned back to Alex. "I didn't know you went to this church."

"New development. The kids joined the youth group. We haven't even visited Sunday services yet." He didn't mention that they attended services at his own church irregularly at best.

"Then you need to give the church a try. Reverend Fraser's the best."

Eli must have said something else after that, something about how great Chestnut Grove Community Church was, but Alex didn't hear it. The only sound filtering into his ears was Dinah's musical laughter, like a tinkling of ice cubes in a tall glass of lemonade.

He heard her before he saw her, sitting in a group of teens and painting a huge sign. Her usually pretty hands were dotted with red poster paint.

"…Dinah Fraser is pretty great, too."

The last brought Alex's head up with a snap. His friend gave him a knowing look. He could only imagine what Eli had seen, but he didn't doubt it was more than he ever intended to reveal.

"So I guess that you've all made some new friends here." Eli's comment wasn't as inane as it would have sounded to someone walking by right then.

"A few."

"Never can have too many friends." Eli smiled like a man with a secret before glancing over at one of the workstations. "I'm helping to caulk the inside of the dunk tank tonight. We had some leakage last year."

"Sounds like a problem," Alex agreed. "Why are you here tonight, anyway? You don't have any teenagers at home."

"A lot of the church members just come in to help the youth center teens get ready for the carnival. They need all the help they can get. Besides, Rachel and I do have a future teenager right over there." He pointed to the tiny lump inside an infant car seat next to the wall.

Alex stepped closer to the car seat and bent to examine the pink-cheeked baby covered with a fuzzy blanket. Tufts of light brown hair poked out from beneath a little pink cap.

"That one looks like a keeper, Eli. What's her name?"

"Madeleine. She's already two months old." Eli

spoke with the pride of a father who'd enjoyed every minute of those first few months.

A sudden stab of envy surprised Alex, but he pushed it to the back of his mind where it belonged. Since when had he started thinking about having children, anyway? Or even dating, for that matter? An obvious answer was since a certain parent-teacher conference, but he tucked that thought away along with the other one.

"There seem to be several pregnant women and a lot of little kids around here. Is this church having a population explosion or what?"

"You sure could call it that," a feminine voice from behind him said.

Alex turned to see Dinah, paint-spattered hands and all. How she could have escaped his notice long enough to sneak up behind him, he wasn't sure.

Eli chuckled. "Rachel, Pilar Fletcher and Kelly Van Zandt even called themselves 'belly buddies' because they were all pregnant together, but my Rachel was the first to drop out of the club. Pilar's next. She's right over there."

He pointed out an olive-skinned woman with raven-colored hair tied in a long ponytail. The rounded tummy of her advanced pregnancy stood out against her trim figure. "Rachel and I and Zach and Pilar were married in a double ceremony two years ago. Now we'll be raising kids together."

"It's great the way God has been blessing the families in our church lately," Dinah told Alex. "These families are growing through births and through adoptions."

With a tilt of her head, she indicated two brown-skinned preschoolers with curly brown hair. They looked to be brother and sister.

"Those two are Adriana and Eduardo," she said. "Zach and Pilar are adopting them through Tiny Blessings."

Alex lifted an eyebrow. "But Pilar's already pregnant."

"The Fletchers want a big family," Eli said, grinning. "In a few years, we'll have to double the size of the youth center to fit all of us."

A strange, stark look appeared in Dinah's eyes, but she shuttered it away, leaving him to wonder if he'd seen it at all. Did Dinah worry that hers would not be among the children to populate the Chestnut Grove church community? Did she long to have a husband and be one of the "belly buddies"? Okay, he doubted she would be clamoring for that particular club membership, but did she someday want a home and a family?

Eli cleared his throat, drawing Alex's attention back to him. Dinah turned back, as well, from watching Eduardo and Adriana scurry through the room.

"Well, that leaky tank is calling me, so I'll see you guys later."

Eli waved as he left, a smirk playing on his lips. Dinah must have missed it because she went on as if no awkwardness had just passed between them.

"How's Chelsea dealing with her punishment?"

Alex studied her. "Why? Did the custodian say she's been doing a bad job?"

"No way. Mr. Vinton said she's such a hard worker that he wished he could hire her as his personal assistant…after her assignment is completed, anyway. I was talking about her punishment at home."

Alex lifted a shoulder and lowered it. "Chelsea's doing fine with it, but I'm about to go crazy."

"What do you mean? Pretty tough on you not having any playdates?" One side of her mouth lifted.

Rolling his eyes, Alex shook his head at her. "Not that. The TV. I can't even put the evening news on when she's in the room. Losing privileges is her consequence, but it's punishing me, as well."

"Then it's a good thing that you're volunteering at the center a lot in the next week because that will give you something to do in all those TV-free hours."

He answered with a frown.

"It looks like Brandon and Chelsea have already gotten to work." She pointed to the far corner of the room.

Chelsea had joined some of the older girls and was busy painting daisies all over a few of the signs. Brandon was bent over a huge plywood board—probably the front of one of the booths—and was using a staple gun to attach lettering to it. A few of the teenage girls had gathered around to admire his handiwork.

"Are you sure they should trust him with a weapon like that?" Alex said.

"He's being careful. He'll lose his fan club if he starts shooting staples into the air." She brushed her painted hands together as if to indicate that the matter was settled. "Now we need to put you to work."

He glanced at the station where Dinah and her red paint had been last, but when he turned back to her, she put a hammer in his hands.

"Over there." She pointed to a few men who were assembling booth sections and other wooden boxes that must have been prize bins or something.

"Are you sure I can handle all that?" He demonstrated his less than practiced use of a hammer.

"If you can put on a bunch of gear and run into a burning building, I figure you can handle pounding a few nails."

"I can't promise any of the boards will be flush."

"That's the beauty of this. None of them have to be. We'll be pulling everything apart again once the carnival is over."

Alex made his way over to the guys, took his assigned pile of wood from a guy who appeared to be in charge and started pounding nails. As he worked, he couldn't help glancing sidelong at Dinah, who had returned to her painting. Messy hands or not, she brushed on the paint with a fluid grace. As he watched her, he wondered if she painted—not signs but still lifes or landscapes or portraits.

He didn't know, and the truth was he knew almost nothing about Dinah Fraser. Sure, there were those obvious things that everyone knew: the dedicated teacher, the preacher's daughter, the volunteer. Then there were the things that everyone saw: the external beauty and the kindness that proved her beauty was more than skin deep.

But what about the rest? What did she think about when she was alone? What did she hope for? What did she believe about God when no one was watching? What did she pray for? Did she ever question God the way he did? Another furtive glance only made him whack his thumb with the hammer. He stuck the damaged digit into his mouth to keep quiet.

No, he didn't know many things about her, but he realized with a shock every bit as surprising as the blow from that hammer that he really wanted to know.

Dinah stood at the back of her packed classroom as "Firefighter Alex" went through the one-minute-and-thirty-second process of putting on his fire gear as part of his Fire Prevention Awareness presentation. She knew it was only a minute and a half because one of the girls in the back of the classroom clasped a stopwatch in her hand and was holding him to his time limit.

Stepping through the bunker pants into the steel-shank boots, and pulling on the short waistcoat made of aramid fibers, Alex whipped into the uniform of his profession with an ease and enthusiasm that didn't suggest this was the fourth presentation he'd given this morning. It was also the fourth time that morning he'd put on and taken off all that gear—*donning and doffing,* he'd called it.

Next he added the hood, mask, helmet with its shield and the SCBA—the self-contained breathing apparatus. His heavy gloves he pulled on last.

"Done. How much time?" He pointed to the second-grader named Kaitlyn who was holding his stopwatch. The mask garbled his words, making his voice sound as if he were speaking in a tunnel and holding marbles in his mouth at the same time.

The child had clicked the stop button at the right time but appeared to be struggling to read the stopwatch, so her teacher leaned over and whispered something in her ear.

"One minute and nineteen seconds," the child announced.

Alex whipped off the helmet and mask. "Hmm, I can do better than that."

Dinah didn't have any doubt that he could and probably *had* at one of his earlier demonstrations. The students, however, seemed to think the performance was just fine, and the room rang out in cheers.

She wanted to cheer, too, but she worried too many people might notice a teacher whooping it up. Still, there was just something about a man in uniform. This was the first time she'd seen Alex in his—the crisp white uniform shirt with a name badge and an insignia on the sleeve, the dark tie and dark slacks.

She had seen him several times in his fire gear, but she'd never had the luxury of being able to study him at her leisure. Now she could just enjoy his presentation as so many other teachers and students had this afternoon.

While she continued to observe, Alex slipped his mask and helmet back on and squeezed among the desks, letting each of the second- and third-graders get a closer look at a firefighter in full gear.

"Did you know all the other gear and the SCBA adds sixty pounds to the firefighter's weight when he or she goes into a fire? That's like me carrying one of you on my back while holding my part of a charged line. That's what we call a hose with water flowing into it. Would any of you want to try to wear all that gear and go into a fire?"

Several boys and girls raised their hands, making Dinah smile. They didn't seem to care about the tough picture he'd painted; they still wanted to be just like Alex when they grew up.

After he removed the gear and was back wearing only his uniform, he got into the true meat of the discussion.

"What happens when you pull fire alarms at your school?"

"We go to prison?" one precocious youngster who'd probably seen one too many episodes of *Law and Order* offered.

"Well, probably not, but I'm going for something different here."

Off to the right, Chelsea raised her hand and waited, but Alex didn't call on his cousin right away. He patiently accepted answers from students who'd raised their hands to suggest anything from "You call our parents" to "The school burns down" before he called on her.

"We might think the next fire alarm is a joke," she said simply.

"That's right, Chelsea."

Dinah had hoped she would get that right, especially since Alex had been pounding that idea into her sweet little head ever since the alarm-pulling incident.

"If someone pulls a fire alarm, the next time we might wonder whether an alarm is real or not rather than focusing on getting out of the building as quickly and as orderly as possible."

A boy on the opposite side of the room raised his hand. "Chelsea pulled the fire alarm."

Dinah tried to hide it, but Alex looked over in time to catch her grinning. Weren't kids great? They were always willing to help out, especially when help involved tattling in some way.

"It's wrong for anyone to pull the alarm," Alex said, rather than address that specific instance. "And when an alarm does go off, even if it's a drill, we must always take it seriously so we can make sure no one gets hurt.

"Can you guys all promise that you'll take every alarm seriously?"

"Yes, Firefighter Alex," his enthralled audience chimed.

"Now, how many of you have a fire escape plan at home?"

A few hands lifted into the air, but from Alex's expression, Dinah could tell it was too few in his opinion.

"Who can tell me what a fire escape plan is?"

One second-grade boy put it succinctly. "It's a plan of how to get your family out if your house is on fire."

Though the children appeared to be riveted on the man as he discussed escape routes and important safety information such as "stop, drop and roll," Dinah's thoughts kept drifting from Alex's words to the man himself.

When it came to the subject of heroes, Alex was the real McCoy. It didn't matter whether he was hauling a heavy hose into a fire or stepping up as caregiver for his cousin's children or even spending a whole day at Grove Elementary, teaching children lessons that could save their lives, he was there and up for the challenge. Was it just the heroism that he exuded like natural, magnetic cologne, or something more that drew her to him and made her begin each day hoping their paths would cross?

Have you ever considered that Chelsea might be right? The principal's words played in her mind as they had more times than was wise in the last few days. What would it be like to date Alex Donovan? Would he be as kind and attentive on a date as he was as a guardian to Brandon and Chelsea or as a presenter to these students? She didn't know if she was ready to attempt the whole dating-relationship thing again, but thoughts of Alex holding her hand or even kissing her made the idea sound downright appealing.

Her thoughts were interrupted when the crowd started applauding, signaling that the presentation had ended. She could only hope that whatever she missed in Alex's speech wouldn't return to embarrass her later.

She was standing at the doorway and directing the last of the second-graders, who'd squeezed into her classroom to share the presentation, back to their own classes when Alex sidled up to her, carrying all of his gear. He set it at his feet and indicated the inside of the classroom with a tilt of his head.

"Hope I wasn't boring you too much there at the end."

"Oh, no." If he only knew. "Your presentation was really interesting."

"Not nearly as compelling for you as whatever you were looking at outside the window."

Her cheeks warmed, both from what he'd said and what he didn't know. "Sorry. It wasn't your speech. I was just sort of drifting." To where, she wasn't about to divulge.

"Thanks for coming, Firefighter Alex. The children will all be fire safety experts now."

"Just what you were hoping for, twenty-four little Smokey Bears running around your class."

"Really. Thanks. My students just loved your presentation, especially the part when you put on your gear."

"That's as much for the firefighters as for the kids."

"How's that?"

"You saw that scary mask, didn't you? How'd you like to be a six-year-old who is awakened at two in the morning by somebody wearing that mask and saying he's going to help you?"

"You're right. That is pretty scary."

"That's why we put on our gear in front of the kids so they'll get familiar with it. We don't want to be *the stranger* to them during a rescue."

Dinah didn't have any doubt that Alex could convince even the most terrified preschooler to trust him, but she didn't tell him that.

"Hey, I was going to suggest that you schedule a field trip to the firehouse sometime soon. The kids would probably get a kick out of touring the station and climbing in the truck."

"Can it be all of the third-grade classes? We like to plan the same field trips."

"As long as everyone knows that I did it for Chelsea. She has to have some special treatment for having to put up with me at home."

"Yes, she does, because that has to be just awful," she teased, smiling. "If you're sure, then I'll put in a request at the office."

She glanced over her shoulder, where her students were still quiet so far, and then turned back to him. Alex was studying his thumbnail, which had turned black.

"What happened there?"

"A casualty of working at the youth center. Maybe you shouldn't have trusted me with that hammer."

"Maybe not." Strange how she was tempted to reach over and touch it, but she decided it wasn't the best idea.

Another peek over her shoulder told her that her students were becoming more rambunctious. From experience, she knew she only had a few minutes before true chaos erupted, but she risked it for the chance to talk with him a little longer.

"Was that your last presentation today?"

"I have one more, to the sixth-graders."

"Ooh, tough crowd." The oldest group, the one that *ruled the school,* wasn't known for its graciousness to guests. In fact, Mrs. Pratt would probably attend that session to help the teachers keep order.

"Thanks for the vote of confidence."

"I didn't say you couldn't handle it."

"Then thanks, at least for not saying I couldn't."

"You know what I meant." But there was mischief in his eyes, so she didn't bother explaining.

"Well, break a leg," she said, as she would to any performer preparing to go onstage. "On second thought, don't."

He laughed at that as he gathered up his gear again and started out the door. A few steps away, he glanced back over his shoulder. "If I happen not to be in the hospital having my femur reset, I'll be bringing the crew to work Saturday at the youth center. Will you be there again?"

"I'm on duty every day until the carnival."

"Then we'll see you there."

The noise in her classroom was growing to a dull roar now, and students who had stayed in their seats for longer than she expected were beginning to get antsy.

Alex followed her gaze and then turned back to her. "Looks like the fire safety experts are getting restless."

She nodded.

He took a few more steps away and then turned back a second time, gesturing for her to step outside the door.

Dinah shot a worried glance into the classroom but couldn't help taking those few steps toward him. "If I don't get in there soon, my classroom's going to combust."

"Before you go, I have another quick question."

"What's that?" she managed, while her pulse hurried along at a pace that couldn't be healthy. She waited, but he didn't say anything right away. If he called this a quick question, she couldn't imagine what he would think was a long one.

"Would you like to have dinner with me tomorrow night?"

"Tomorrow night?" she croaked. Her palms were suddenly sweaty—a reminder of how far out of the dating loop she'd been in the last few years.

"Why? Is another night better?"

"No. Tomorrow's fine."

"Good. Then it's a date. I'll pick you up at seven." He was grinning at her now.

Dinah cleared her throat and demanded that her squirming insides become still that instant. She had a question of her own that needed answering. "Don't you think it would be rewarding Chelsea's bad behavior for us to go out now, after everything?"

He moved his head to one side and then to the other as if considering. "I've thought about that, and I'm sure it is to some degree."

"Then should we just for—"

"Forget it?" he finished for her. "Do you really want to forget it, Miss Fraser?"

Now that wasn't fair. Not only did he look at her with eyes that could have swayed even a Supreme Court justice, but even the way he said her name was like another appeal. She chewed her lip and then shook her head.

"Me, neither," he said, his smile kind. "I realize our going out might reward Little Miss Matchmaker, but our not going out would be just like the TV."

"Like the TV, how?"

"Remember when I said that taking away Chelsea's television privilege felt like it was punishing me, as well?" He waited on her nod before he continued. "Well, our not getting the chance to know each other better would be just like that. It would be punishing *us*."

Chapter Seven

Alex parked across the street from an unassuming tan brick colonial, crossed his arms over the steering wheel and buried his face in the middle. *Could this day get any worse?* He lifted his head up from the pile formed by his arms. Maybe he shouldn't ask.

"Are you just going to sit there, or are you going to go get her?" Brandon asked from the backseat where he was probably still sulking with his arms folded over his chest.

Brandon had been brooding ever since Alex had picked him up from school detention earlier. The call that Brandon had earned the after-school privilege hadn't exactly been the high point of the night.

It had gone downhill from there. A babysitter debacle and one brand-new scorched dress shirt later, here he was. Here they all were.

"Yeah, Uncle Alex, she's waiting for you." Unlike her brother, Chelsea was bouncing in the seat, so much so that the car rocked.

"I'm going. Just give me a minute." Alex took a deep breath and unfastened his safety belt. Some date this was shaping up to be—that was if she still agreed to go once she heard his tale of woe. Steadying himself, he climbed out of the car and crossed the street.

Though it had at first appeared ordinary, the house before him seemed to exude warmth. Everything about it was inviting, from the oval-shaped window in the front door that refracted light from inside to the mature oaks on either side of the house.

He continued up the walk, past a planter of yellow mums on the steps, and stopped at the door. It flew open before he had a chance to ring the bell, but instead of the auburn-haired beauty he was expecting, a pretty young woman with copper hair and a dusting of freckles looked out at him.

"You must be Alex." She waved him inside and closed the door behind him. "I'm Dinah's sister, Ruth. Her much younger sister, of course.

"I go to Hollins University, a women's college in Roanoke, but I'm home for the weekend."

Because she hadn't taken a single breath until then, Alex spoke while he had the chance. "It's nice to meet you. Is Dinah here?" He glanced around the house that looked just as comfortable on the inside as it had outside. It had a clean but lived-in look that reminded him of his childhood home.

"Sure, she's upstairs, trying to make an entrance and all of that, you know." She paused long enough to give him a critical once-over. "Dinah's right. You're pretty hunky."

"Ruth Fraser, come in the kitchen this instant," came a voice from farther inside the house.

"Sure, Mom." The young woman glanced over her shoulder and then, turning back to Alex, she shrugged. "She thinks I'm boy crazy," she said, before sauntering down the hall.

Naomi Fraser was probably right about that, and he had an idea why Ruth was attending a women's college, but Alex figured it wouldn't be a good idea to say so. That was all he needed, to add offending Dinah's family to everything else that had gone wrong today.

So much for the romantic dinner for two that he'd been looking forward to all day.

Naomi appeared from the kitchen then, wiping her hands on a dish towel. She grabbed him for a hug with the practiced hands of someone comfortable hugging everyone.

"You'll have to forgive our Ruth, Alex. She gets a little overenthusiastic."

"She's fine. Good kid."

"Ruth's that, all right." Naomi chuckled. "Sorry that John can't be here to meet with you. He's in his study, working on Sunday's sermon, but…"

She let her words fall away as a door creaked open. Reverend Fraser appeared in the hallway, his glasses perched on the end of his nose. "No, I'm here, my dear. I wouldn't miss this chance to have a few words with Dinah's young man."

Young man? Alex hoped the minister was joking, but Reverend Fraser kept a straight face.

"It's nice to see you again, Alex." He offered his hand.

Alex gripped it, wondering if he should remind Dinah's father that he'd been an adult for well over a decade. "Good to see you, too."

"So, what are your plans for tonight?"

"That's up to your daughter, sir," Alex answered vaguely. They might not be going out at all, depending on what she decided, but he didn't mention that. If the minister asked him about his intentions regarding Dinah, he would die of embarrassment right then and there.

John opened his mouth to say more, but Naomi crossed to him and placed her hand on his arm.

"I wonder what's taking Dinah so long," she said. "They probably need to get going or they'll be late for dinner."

The reservation, Alex thought with a grimace. He'd felt so privileged to get one at the last minute at the fancy steak house he could barely afford, and now he had to cancel it.

A creak from above drew their attention to the stairs. The woman descending from the second floor took Alex's breath away. Dinah had fussed with her appearance, wearing a soft-looking sweater and a long, filmy skirt with flowers all over it. She'd arranged her hair in one of those fancy updos, leaving a few pieces down, soft about her face. He'd never seen her looking prettier or more feminine.

"Wow." The word just escaped him before he had a chance to censor himself. After a reaction like that, there was no way the minister would let him out of the house with his daughter, even with chaperones.

The color of Dinah's cheeks deepened, but she smiled. "You're not interrogating my date, are you, Dad?"

"He was trying, but I stopped him in time," Naomi said with a chuckle that gave a hint where Dinah got her musical laugh.

As she reached the landing, she glanced at Alex again, and her gaze narrowed as she took in his jeans, brown leather jacket, rugby shirt and tennis shoes. "Am I overdressed? I thought you said this place was dressy."

"That's what I was going to talk to you about." He'd been dreading this moment all night, and he felt just as lousy as he'd known he would, but he hadn't expected the words to come so hard.

Finally, he took her arm and directed her to look out the front window. From across the street, they still would have been able to see Brandon and Chelsea sitting in the backseat, but it was much more obvious since Chelsea had rolled down the window and was hanging out it, waving.

Dinah looked sidelong at Alex. "Was that dinner reservation for four?"

Alex blew out a breath that underscored his frustration. "No, just two. But I know now why parents complain so much about babysitters. First, my neighbor who's always available to sit…wasn't. Then the college girl my neighbor suggested must have received a better offer because she canceled at the last minute."

She'd turned back to him, and her smile spread as he told his story.

"Sounds like you've had a rough night."

"You don't know the half of it."

"Well, that's too bad." She turned her chin up and studied him as if she'd be willing to hear the rest of what happened, giving Alex another reason to like her. Lately, he was finding more reasons than he could count.

"None of it has to ruin tonight, though. I doubt the fancy restaurant would work, but the four of us could get a pizza or something. Or if you'd rather just reschedule…" He wished he couldn't hear the hope in his voice. He didn't like being vulnerable, and he didn't want to start now.

"I've got to go upstairs."

Dinah turned and jogged up the stairs, not looking back even once. Alex stared after her until she reached the upper level, and then he looked at her parents.

"Now what just happened?" He'd known when he'd shown up there and suggested alternative plans that there was a chance she would say no, but he wasn't prepared for this reaction. Was this her way of saying no? Had she just trucked upstairs to see how long he would stand around waiting until he got the hint and left?

Reverend Fraser shrugged and pushed his glasses up on his nose. "Your guess is as good as mine. Women. You'd think I would have figured them out after all of these years, but, sadly, no. God has made them a delightful puzzle, hasn't He?"

Naomi rolled her eyes and elbowed her husband in the side. "Delightful, all right. All I know is I raised these children to have some manners, and they've all forgotten them."

Ruth chose that moment to return from the kitchen, where she'd been temporarily banished.

"Aw, don't worry, Mom." She slipped in next to Naomi and wrapped an arm around her shoulder. "We have those nice manners you were working so hard to instill in us. Even Jonah. We just do a good job at hiding them."

Ruth planted a kiss on her mother's cheek, and though Naomi frowned at her outspoken daughter, she kissed her back.

John's hearty chuckle filled the room. "You see. They're quite a puzzle."

The sound of footsteps brought back everyone's attention to the stairs. Now sporting a pair of jeans, a sweater and tennis shoes, Dinah looked as lovely as before, if a lot more comfortable. She had a jacket over her arm. Her pretty hairdo she'd tugged down and pulled into a regular ponytail, but the little wisps of hair at her cheeks remained.

"What's going on, everyone?"

Curiosity lit Dinah's eyes, but Alex had his own question to ask. "You're coming with us?"

"Of course I'm coming. Why are you asking that?"

Alex shrugged. "When you said you had to go upstairs, I thought—"

"That I didn't want to go?" She looked at him as if that thought was ludicrous. "Of course I'm going. I happen to love pizza."

Reverend Fraser clapped his hands together. "Glad we have that settled. Two chaperones are a great addition to the evening, in my opinion."

Dinah directed a frown her father's way as Alex

helped her into her jacket. "Do I need to remind you that I'm twenty-five years old?"

He tilted his head to the side. "You'll always be my little girl."

Instead of bristling at her father's comment, Dinah smiled. "I know, Daddy." She stepped over to him and kissed his cheek.

It was a sweet gesture between father and daughter, but Alex couldn't help wondering what it would be like to be the privileged recipient of her kiss. He was still imagining that gift when Dinah crossed back to him and took his arm.

"Now it's time to eat some serious pizza. Did I mention that I could eat my weight in pizza?"

He patted her arm with his free hand. "My kind of girl."

Though he'd meant it as a joke, the truth in his words struck him. Only Dinah Fraser could be equally delighted with a pizza foursome as with a dinner for two. He liked that about her, that she could see the fun in any situation. She looked at her world with the bright eyes of a child, when his own eyes had been jaded and dull for too long.

Perhaps it was this joie de vivre that drew him to her, or perhaps it was something more difficult to pinpoint. All he was certain of was that he was more excited for this date-for-four than he'd ever been for a date before.

"Five whole dollars? Apiece?"

Chelsea's eyes had to be the size of silver dollars, but she was quick to grasp the two five-dollar bills that

Alex waved in front of her and to hand one of them to her brother. Brandon had managed to stay sullen all through the pepperoni with extra cheese, but he perked up at the prospect of a video-induced stupor. He took his bill and they rushed off in search of a token machine.

Dinah followed their departure with her gaze until they'd reached the pizza parlor's game room, and then she turned back to Alex. They still weren't really alone, but the idea of a few stolen minutes, just the two of them, made her hands sweaty.

"That went well," she said with a smile.

"I know. I know. Bribing children would rank up at the top of the 'don't' list in any parenting guide."

"I didn't say anything."

"But you thought it."

"I didn't even think it." No, her thoughts had been on things other than his parenting skills or even the children.

"Hey, thanks for being so cool about it when I had to change our plans. I expected you to cancel when you saw the kids. A lot of women would have."

"Not me."

An unreadable emotion passed over his face, and then he nodded.

"And most women haven't gone as long as I have without a date."

"That long, eh?"

"Long enough that I had been considering being one of the first guinea pigs for a new online Christian dating service. Have you heard about it? It's my mom's brainchild."

"I hadn't heard about it, but I can picture your mom

coming up with the idea. She seems like a real mover and shaker." He poked at the lone piece of pizza crust still on his plate. "Now your dad, I can see how he would be tough on a daughter's social life. He's a little overprotective, isn't he?"

"As he said, I'll always be his little girl." She shrugged. "He just doesn't want me to get hurt."

Alex nodded. "Wait, you said *had been considering* trying out your mom's online dating service. Does that mean you've changed your mind?"

Now how was she supposed to answer that? Should she tell him that it wouldn't be fair to any of the dynamic Christian men she could meet through the online service when she would only compare them to a certain firefighter with dark, intelligent eyes and a hero complex? Would he want to hear that, for the time being, anyway, she didn't want to meet anyone else? Coward that she was, Dinah opted for an easy way out.

"Since this dating-with-kid-chaperones thing sounded like the newest social craze, I decided to try it out for a while."

"For a while?"

"A few hours, anyway," she said with a shrug.

Alex glanced to the game area, where Chelsea sat perched on a stationary racing motorcycle with Brandon just behind the rear tire, offering direction. "Well, right now this appears to be a one-on-one date. For the next...ah—" he peeked at his watch "—twenty minutes or so, until they run out of tokens and come begging for more."

"Then we'd better hurry up and have fun."

"I don't know about you; but I'm having fun already."

His smile was so warm that it felt as if he'd touched her without even moving his hand. "Me, too," she managed to say over the tightness in her throat.

"It was worth ten dollars to get a break from Brandon's scowl for a while."

She recognized it as a weak attempt to lighten the intensity of the moment, but she decided to let him get away with it. "What was all of Brandon's brooding about, anyway?"

"He had detention today for calling his history teacher an idiot." He wore that same disappointed frown that had been on his face as he'd dealt with Chelsea after the false alarm.

"Why do you think he called him that?"

Alex reached for the last piece of pizza that Dinah guessed wouldn't even have been there if Brandon had been acting, or more specifically, eating, like himself. After Alex took a bite, chewed and swallowed, he tilted his head to the side. "You mean besides that his teacher is an—"

"Yeah, besides that."

"Oh yeah, you're a teacher, too." He was grinning as he said it, but then he became serious. "I don't know why he said it. I can only assume that he's still acting out because he's worried about his mom and dad."

She swallowed, remembering. For a few minutes she could forget about the worries Alex, Chelsea and Brandon shared, but those three couldn't ever forget.

"At least he has an excuse for his crazy behavior. Most of us just have to chalk it up to surviving our irrational teen years."

"That sounds like it comes from experience, but somehow I can't imagine you being an *irrational teen*."

It was Dinah's turn to smile. "You mean because I'm a preacher's daughter? Haven't you ever heard about preachers' kids who get into trouble?"

"Sure, I have. But somehow I don't think you did."

"I didn't make the newspaper police blotter, if that's what you're thinking qualifies a person as a rebellious teen, but I was a bit of a wild child in my own way. I just didn't do it in public."

Alex rested his forearms on the table and leaned forward, appearing interested. "So what did you do in private to make you this *wild child?*"

She bristled at the way one corner of his mouth lifted. "Hey, it's true. When I had friends sleep over, I would drive my parents crazy by blaring heavy-metal music late into the night. It wasn't the kind of music they wanted me listening to, either."

"Don't worry. I wasn't much of a rebel, either."

"I wasn't finished," she said with a frown. "I even experimented with the idea of being an agnostic in high school, but, thankfully, that phase was short-lived."

At that, Alex shook his head vehemently. "You, an agnostic? I can't believe it."

"When your parents are people of faith, especially people who are so public about their faith, what is the one thing you can do that hurts them the most? You question whether or not God exists."

"You seem pretty active in the Chestnut Grove Church now. How did you find your answer?"

"My dad would be the obvious guess, but it was really Mom who helped me to see the truth. She sat me down one night and told me I could choose to believe whatever I wanted to, but there was nothing I could do that would convince her that God *didn't* exist.

"She said His miracles in her life had spoken for themselves, and then she named them. First Jonah, then me, and, finally, Ruth. I was questioning everything she held dear, and still she called *me* a miracle."

Alex reached for the pitcher and poured more cola in his glass. "I'm surprised she didn't say that you were a test from God."

"I was a test, all right." She shook her head, picturing that teenage girl she no longer was.

"If that isn't ironic, I don't know what is."

"What's that?"

"Compared to you—the PK—I must have been a piece of cake for my parents to raise. I turned the music down when they asked me to. I came home before curfew. I even went to church every Sunday without complaining too much."

His eyes took on a faraway look for a few seconds, and whatever he saw made him smile. "Karla used to torture me because her parents kept asking her why she couldn't be more like me."

"Boy, your folks did have it easy."

His jaw tightened then, and his eyes took on a steel-like quality. "Even leaders in corrupt governments know that it's easier to keep citizens in line if you keep them in the dark about their secrets. George and Edie had to know it, too. Maybe they wouldn't have had such a cakewalk raising me if they'd told me about—" He shook his head hard, as if to cast away whatever he'd been about to say.

"About what?"

Alex blinked a few times, realizing what he'd almost said. "It's nothing. Forget it."

He hadn't talked to anyone about discovering he was adopted except Karla and that private investigator. He'd told Karla the details when he'd found his birth records, but Alex had never told anyone about the betrayal he'd felt. Today he'd been tempted to share it all with Dinah, and he didn't know what to think about that.

What was he so afraid of? None of it was his fault. His parents had made that decision not to tell, and they had died never having to face the consequences of their choice. Would Dinah see him as a victim here, or would she see what he saw when he looked in the mirror in the morning: a man who didn't have a clue who he was anymore?

Dinah opened her mouth as if to ask the question Alex wasn't ready to answer, but just then Chelsea and Brandon came rushing back to the table.

"Uncle Alex, we're all out of tokens." Chelsea held out her empty hands for effect. "Can we have some more money? Please."

"Yeah, please, Alex," Brandon chimed. "There's this really cool race car game, and I'm this close to earning top score." He held his thumb and forefinger about a half inch apart to demonstrate just how close he was to this amazing achievement.

Alex and Dinah stared at each other, each lifting an eyebrow. Clearly, video game therapy was working for Brandon.

"I don't know. What do you think, Miss Fraser? Should I let them have some more money?"

Chelsea put on her worried face that she used whenever she had to think of grown-up concerns. "Do you have any more money?"

"Oh, I think I have a few more dollars I can spare without breaking the bank." He reached into his wallet and withdrew a ten-dollar bill. "Now when this is gone, we'll be going home, so don't ask me for any more."

"Okay. Thanks, Uncle Alex." Chelsea bounced over to him and, wrapping her arms around him, planted a kiss on his cheek.

"Yeah, thanks."

Brandon didn't offer hugs and kisses as his sister had, but he almost smiled, and that was enough. In a flash, the brother and sister were off again to race at lightning speeds and conquer new worlds.

When Alex turned back to Dinah, she grinned. "All this bribing is getting expensive."

"Don't I know it," he said, pausing before adding, "but it's worth it for fifteen more minutes."

He didn't add *alone with you,* but he knew it was understood. She seemed to crave these private moments as much as he did. He couldn't get enough, of watching her graceful movements, of breathing in the light floral scent of her perfume.

His fingers itched to reach out and touch one of those little wisps of hair at her cheek. He'd already lifted his hand to do just that when she glanced over at the children and then quickly turned back to him. He lowered his hand.

"Hey, you said Brandon had detention today. Did you just let that be his punishment, or did he have additional consequences at home?"

"There were more. No TV and no Internet—except for homework—for two weeks."

She nodded. "You definitely have the whole loss of privileges thing down."

"But at some point I'm going to have to stop taking away TV as a consequence. If the two of them keep messing up this way, I'll never get to watch the evening news again."

She laughed at that, her eyes crinkling at the corners. "You'll probably be up in the middle of the night watching infomercials just to get to see that flickering screen."

"What do you mean flickering screen? I have a forty-two-inch plasma at my house. It knows better than to *flicker.*"

"You're such a guy," she said, shaking her head.

"You say that like it's a bad thing."

"It's not."

Again, she was smiling at him, and he realized he would say almost anything to make her look that happy.

As if by tacit agreement, they both stood up from the table and made their way over to the game area for the last few minutes before the tokens disappeared again. Chelsea took two more rides on the motorcycle that went nowhere, and Brandon managed to earn that elusive top score on his last token. Dinah cheered them both on though it was clear that she and video games didn't speak the same language.

When there were no more excuses to stall, they piled into his SUV and returned to the Fraser home. Alex opened the car door for Dinah and helped her out, but, aware of their audience still inside the car, he released her hand as soon as she was on her feet. His hands ached so much to reach for her again that he stuffed them in his jacket pockets to stop himself.

Instead, he shuffled up the walk beside her, and she matched his pace, seeming to understand his reluctance to hurry. Though this date hadn't turned out anything like what he'd planned, he still didn't want it to end. As they stopped at the bottom of the porch steps under the glow of the outdoor light, he half expected Reverend Fraser to be watching them, but the curtains didn't even flutter.

"Your dad must be slipping on the job here," he said, pointing to the oval window in the center of the front door. "Where is he?"

"Mom probably wrestled him to the floor or he'd be up here flashing the front-porch light off and on right now."

He could picture that and was grateful for Dinah's spunky mother, who seemed to have passed her strength and humor along to both of her daughters. As he turned, Alex's gaze came to rest on the sweet face of Naomi's oldest daughter, and he couldn't bring himself to look away.

"Mom can only hold Dad on the floor for so long, though. Nobody's wrestling skills are that good."

"Oh. Right." Clearing his throat, he pressed his fists farther into his pockets. "I just wanted to say once more how sorry I am about tonight."

"Don't be. I had a wonderful time."

"Me, too. Still, I want to make it up to you. You already said you'd be working on carnival stuff all day tomorrow. How about next Saturday?"

"Did you forget?" She drew her eyebrows together and studied him. "Saturday *is* the carnival. And we'll be working every night up until then on the booths, and that Saturday we'll probably be up to our elbows in cotton candy."

"You're right. After the carnival. How about next Sunday night? Oh. Right. Sunday evening services."

Alex couldn't help frowning. He wanted to see her again, to really be alone with her this time, and, though he liked the idea of seeing her at the youth center every day until then, it wasn't enough.

"Hold that thought." She paused, closing her eyes and tapping her index finger against her lips as if deep in thought. "No. Sunday's good. Dad said he would be canceling the evening service so everyone could spend time with their families after all this work to put the carnival together."

"Then Sunday night it is."

That he felt as giddy as one of Dinah's students when a snow day was called should have shamed him, but it didn't. They would have to wait for it, but it gave him the time to plan a dinner date she would never forget.

Then a thought crossed his mind that rained all over

his parade and left all the imaginary floats sopping wet. "Won't you be expected to spend time with *your* family during this free family evening?"

Dinah rolled her eyes at him. "The Fraser household is going to have to do without me just this once." Glancing at the window to see if they'd gained another audience from inside the house, she turned back to him and winked. "I happen to have an important date that night."

An important date? This was supposed to be casual, just a laid-back opportunity for two adults to get to know each other better. But he recognized that he'd been kidding himself to have ever thought so. A date with Dinah Fraser would never be a laid-back event for him.

When he wanted nothing more than to take her in his arms in front of God and relatives and anyone else watching, Alex extended his hand to her, and she gripped it in a polite handshake. If nothing else had been normal about this date, at least he would end it as the type of gentleman Dinah deserved.

"Thanks again." After a few seconds, Dinah withdrew her hand from his. "Will I see you at church this Sunday, or will you be attending services at your own church?"

"Probably mine."

She smiled and nodded, but he sensed she didn't believe him. As seldom as he'd attended lately, he didn't quite believe himself.

"Well, good night." She turned to wave at the children in the car before tripping up the steps to go inside.

"Good night."

Alex watched after her for a few seconds and then turned and strode back down the walk. He was still smiling when he opened the door to the SUV.

"Why didn't you kiss her, Uncle Alex?"

He sighed but didn't answer. He should have expected a comment like that from Chelsea, who probably had high hopes for this date that she'd orchestrated.

She was too young to recognize it, but this date that hadn't been sealed with a kiss had been more successful than she knew. He wasn't ready to tell her, either. He wasn't ready to admit that he couldn't wait for their second date or for every minute he would spend with Dinah until then as they prepared for the carnival. Some things were meant to be private.

For once Alex was grateful for Brandon's brooding personality. At least he wouldn't have to face some embarrassing comment from a boy who was almost old enough to understand some of the things Alex was feeling.

Slipping the keys back in the ignition, Alex started the engine and put the car in Drive. As he peeked into his rearview mirror to check for oncoming traffic, he caught sight of the boy who often looked anywhere but at him. This time, though, Brandon was staring right his way.

"Yeah, Alex, why didn't you kiss her?"

Chapter Eight

J ared Kierney settled into the comfortable guest chair in the office for Cavanaugh Carpentry, located in the downstairs of Ben and Leah Cavanaugh's cozy, three-bedroom home. Unfortunately, the man who carried cups of coffee for himself and Jared into the room didn't appear as relaxed as his surroundings. Far from it.

"Thanks, Ben." Jared took a sip of the too-strong brew and managed to swallow it before setting the cup on the coaster Ben had provided. "That hits the spot."

"You're too kind."

Ben's ironic smile hinted that he might be able to relax during this meeting with the help of a seasoned reporter, and Jared was just the guy to do it. He knew plenty of tricks for putting his interview subjects at ease.

"You're right, I am too kind. Have you ever *made* coffee before?"

Ben took a sip from his own coffee and grimaced.

"Not often enough. Leah's so much better at making it that we agreed it would be her job." He shrugged. "Tonight, she took Olivia and the baby to the Starlight Diner for dinner, so we could…do this."

By "do this," Ben meant that they would discuss the intensely private matters regarding his falsified birth records and the search for his birth mother for an article in the *Richmond Gazette*. Jared figured a little more small talk would be necessary to set Ben at ease.

"How is Olivia dealing with the arrival of little Joseph? It had to be hard becoming a big sister after nine years of being the one and only."

Ben's smile answered for him before his words had a chance. "We were told to expect a little tension, but Olivia fell in love with her baby brother from the first night we let her hold him."

"Chance and Luke were the same way when Hope was born. They think of her as this little redheaded doll." He figured there would never be a perfect time to segue to the subject of his interview, but Jared went with it anyway. "I wanted to thank you again for agreeing to speak to me about your adoption for the article."

Ben shrugged. "If it can help somebody else…"

"I know it will," Jared assured him.

"I hope so."

Jared cleared his throat and studied his prepared list of questions. He hated to bring up difficult memories, but it was the only way he could do justice to Ben's story.

"For the article, let's start at the beginning. When did you first know that you were adopted?"

Ben planted his elbows on his desk, and he stared past Jared instead of at him. His lips lifted. "A better question would be when didn't I know. My parents— Tyrone and Peggy Cavanaugh—" he paused, his gaze flicking to Jared "—talked about adoption all the time, even before I knew what it meant.

"Mom used to say that another woman carried me in her belly, but I was the child of her heart." A sheepish look appeared on the carpenter's face. "Any chance I could get you not to quote me on that?"

Jared chuckled, imagining how emasculating such a comment could appear in print. "It's always my policy to tell the people I interview that nothing's off the record. But if you give me dozens of other great quotes, I'll consider not using that one."

"Thanks, buddy."

"Glad I could help." Jared would have liked to continue the light banter with his friend, but they had a more difficult topic to discuss. "When did you first realize that your birth records were among those that were tampered with at Tiny Blessings Adoption Agency?"

"Not long after the first batch of doctored records were discovered at the office. Until then, I'd always thought my birth parents had a no-contact agreement to keep me from ever reuniting with them.

"Anyway, private investigator Ross Van Zandt told Kelly Young and me that one of us had to be the child of his client. Her baby had been stolen thirty-five years before."

Ben didn't have to go into further detail on that story. They both were well aware now that the client, Sandra

Lange, turned out to be Kelly's birth mother, and former mayor Gerald Morrow was her birth father.

"How did you feel then when you learned that your real records were among the set found at the Harcourt mansion?"

Even as he asked the question, Jared hated himself for having to do it. Why had he thought this series was a good idea in the first place? He'd told himself that sharing the personal side of the adoption scandals would help provide healing and understanding for the victims. Now dredging up these painful memories only seemed cruel.

Ben spun in his executive chair until he faced the window, but after several long seconds, he turned back to his desk. "I don't know. Probably relieved at first. And then excited. I really wanted to meet her."

"You mean your birth mother—" he paused, looking at his question list "—Millicent Cunningham-Watson?" At Ben's nod Jared continued, "I'm sorry to hear she passed away before you had the chance to know her."

"I'm sorry, too." Ben straightened in his seat and planted his hands on the edge of his desk. "I'm also sorry that Barnaby Harcourt used my existence to blackmail her out of a good chunk of the Cunningham Publishing empire's money."

"It has to be hard knowing that."

"You have no idea."

And that was the truth. Jared could only guess at the guilt Ben had to feel for a situation over which he'd had no control—then or now. Ben had that distant look again, as if he was retreating into his thoughts, just when Jared needed him to open up about his adoption.

"Would you rather that the records were never found?"

"Well…" He paused for a long time, considering. "No. I would still want to know. It's one of those enigmas that many children of adoption face. We know that we were wanted by our adoptive parents, but a little part of us can't let go of the fact that, for whatever reason, our birth parents didn't want us."

"Did learning about your birth mother help you answer that question in your mind?"

"It did." Ben settled back in his seat, loosely crossing his arms and appearing relaxed for the first time since the interview began. "I learned that, whatever mistakes Millicent—Millie, they called her—made, she always regretted her decision to give me up for adoption."

Jared felt himself relax, as well. Perhaps Ben's story would help heal a few hearts, after all.

"Though your birth mother had already passed away, did you have the chance to meet anyone else in your extended birth family?"

He already knew the answer to that, but he wanted to give Ben the chance to tell the rest of his story. If he could describe the glowing smile that settled on Ben's face then, Jared would be thrilled with his article when it went into print.

"I found out that in addition to my brother Eli, I have three other brothers and sisters in Maryland."

Jared hated to ask it, but it was the question that adoptive parents had to face eventually—himself and Meg included since the twins, Chance and Luke, were adopted. "How have your adoptive parents felt about your discovery of your birth family?"

"Hey, they're my parents. Nothing can change that. I told them that as soon as Ross told me they'd found my original birth records, and I think Mom and Dad realize it's the truth."

Ben swept his hand wide to indicate his surroundings. "Look at this place. It's the house I grew up in, and I chose to raise my family here when my parents retired to Florida. My memories are here. This place represents my family. My real family."

"Do you think you'll be as understanding if Olivia someday wants to find her birth father?" Jared worded the question carefully because Olivia's adoption was unusual in that Ben was now married to his daughter's birth mother.

"How could I not be? I know I'll be able to relate to Olivia's need to understand where she came from because I'll know that I am just as much a part of who she is as her biological father. Leah will help me if I get sensitive about it." He grinned at the last.

The sound of an opening door and the pounding of running feet turned their attention to the den's doorway.

"We're home, Daddy." A little girl with light brown hair rushed into the room and into her father's lap. "We had pie at the Starlight."

"If it was banana cream, I'm jealous," Ben told her.

"It was banana cream." She giggled with delight.

"Olivia, aren't you supposed to be getting a bath?" Leah stood in the doorway, holding a sleeping infant in her arms. Her smile was warm as she watched her husband nuzzling their daughter.

Jared flipped closed his spiral-topped reporter's

notebook, the perfect ending for his feature article already in his mind. The Cavanaugh family had just given him the reminder he needed and would reinforce with his newspaper series. Families didn't come about by genetics alone. They were formed by love.

"If you're planning to pull a Michelangelo on the *W,* you're never going to make it to the *E* before we quit tonight."

Dinah looked up from where she was kneeling above the weathered Welcome sign, her red-paint-covered brush poised for another stroke. Not that she'd needed to look up to know who stood behind her, even before he spoke. She'd had a sixth sense all week when it came to Alex, and again she'd sensed his nearness. That the skin on her upper arms tingled every time he was within ten feet of her offered a strong clue.

Alex grinned down at her before taking another swallow from his bottled water.

"Art critics are not *welcome,*" she said with a frown.

"Hey, I'm not criticizing the quality of the work, just the pace."

"What would the Sistine Chapel look like if Michelangelo was rushed like this?" With her sleeve, she brushed at the perspiration dotting her forehead.

"I don't know, but I don't think we have several years to spare when the carnival is just two days away."

Dinah stuck out her tongue and then tilted her head to the side. "You know…isn't there an old saying, 'If you want something done right, then do it yourself'?" She extended the brush his way.

Instead of coming up with another quip, Alex pulled a clean paintbrush from his back pocket. "I thought you'd never ask."

Retrieving a bowl, he poured a small amount of paint from her can into it. He pointed to the *E* at the end of the Welcome sign. "I'll start there, and we can meet someplace in the middle—if you get a move on that is."

"Good thing for you there's no quality inspector on the job here."

"Are you saying I do shoddy work?"

Dinah shook her head. There was no way she could say that about a man who took on every project he was given with intensity and a strong work ethic. It didn't matter if he was shirring the material around the table for the pie-throwing booth or reinforcing the braces for the dunk tank, Alex would make sure the job was done right.

"Well, glad to hear it because I was about to be offended."

Alex moved the drop cloth so it could double as a kneeling pad of sorts, settled on it and stuck his brush in the paint.

Dinah waited until he'd taken his first stroke before she began a conversation. "It's probably been a boring week for you at the fire station."

Instead of answering, he looked over at her quizzically.

"You know," she explained. "Not a single alarm from Grove Elementary all week."

He returned to his work with quick, efficient strokes. "That's what we were hoping for when I conducted all those Fire Prevention Awareness presentations." He looked up again and pinned her in his stare. "At least I thought that was what we were both hoping for."

She waved away his comment with a flick of her brush and then scanned the floor, hoping she hadn't spattered the paint. "Of course that's what I want. I was just worried about the guys at the station. You probably miss us."

"Maybe a little," he said with a sigh.

They'd been able to see each other every night this week except Sunday, which, to some extent, made up for the new lack of daytime sightings. Whether they were working together, touching up the paint on signs, or on opposite sides of the room counting prize inventory, Dinah hadn't been able to keep her eyes off him.

The best part—even if it had been a little scary—was that every time she'd glanced at him, she caught him staring back. Even now she smiled over the challenge the distraction had presented. It was downright tough sharing secret glances without getting paint in her hair.

"Come on, Picasso, pick up the pace."

Dinah looked up from where she was doing a fine job on the first *E* in *welcome,* if she did say so herself, to find Alex already finished with his *M* and halfway around the circle of his *O*. They were getting closer to each other by the paint stroke. "First Michelangelo and now Picasso? Aren't you mixing up your genres here?"

"That and time periods. Renaissance and Cubism."

A brawny firefighter who also knew something about art—when was Alex Donovan going to quit surprising her? There was so much to like about Alex, beyond the fact that he'd faced her parents and still seemed to think she was worth the effort.

Alex was different from any of the men she'd known before. Though his strength and confidence had drawn her to him in the first place, it was his caring qualities and his steadfastness that tempted her to step even closer. That in itself should have sent her running in the other direction. She knew better, but she couldn't seem to keep herself from wanting to know him better.

She dipped her brush into the paint and began another series of strokes. "It looks like all this work has been good for Brandon and Chelsea." She glanced around the room, pausing first on Brandon, who was having a little too much fun tossing around stuffed bears that were supposed to be prizes with Tyler. Then she paused on Chelsea, who was spending more time looking adoringly at the big girls than counting bags of hot dog buns. Alex followed the path of her gaze.

"It's keeping their minds off their parents, at least for a little while."

"Have you heard anything new?"

"Karla called yesterday and talked to both of them before she talked to me. She sounded so weak. She still isn't responding to the chemotherapy. She's starting to lose hope."

Dinah wondered if Alex's cousin wasn't the only one. "It will happen." She said it with a certainty she hoped was contagious. "We'll both just keep praying. Any word about Mike's leave from Iraq?"

He only shook his head. "In fact, no word at all for the last four days. Until then, I'd been getting regular e-mails from him. Neither of the kids have thought to ask, and I haven't mentioned it."

Four days without contact. Dinah swallowed. They both knew what that could mean for this family. "Maybe Mike's just on a covert operation or communications are down or something."

"Maybe."

"That's it. I'm sure of it." Before Alex could say he wasn't so sure, Dinah pressed on, shifting the subject. "It takes a special person to enter the military—and to be a firefighter. You never told me why you did it."

Whatever dark thoughts had been crossing his mind seemed to filter away as his posture softened. "What can I say? I have a hero complex."

Since she'd once thought the same thing about him, Dinah couldn't help grinning. "That's it? I figured you lost your kitty in a tree once, a ladder truck came racing down the street, and—"

Alex was already shaking his head. "No, nothing as romantic as that. It's just that, you see, my parents were older when I was born." He cleared his throat and started again. "Anyway, Dad was a firefighter. He had to retire when I was little because of an injury, but he would always tell these incredible stories about heroes who laid their lives on the line for others. Mom and Dad taught me there was honor in that."

"I agree," she said before she could stop herself.

He smiled when she looked over at him again, but it was a sad smile. Was there something more to his story that he wasn't telling?

"I don't know about you, but I think it's kind of a romantic notion to want to follow in your father's footsteps." His noncommittal shrug only made her wonder more. "You must really miss them now that your parents are both gone."

"How'd you know they were gone?"

"You keep forgetting that I'm Chelsea's teacher. I always tell parents that if they'll believe only half of what their children tell them after school, I'll believe only half of the stories their kids tell me from home."

"Still planning on Sunday night?"

"Of course." She wouldn't tell him she'd thought of little else any more than she would inform him that his change of subject couldn't have been more obvious if he'd painted it on a sign. He'd let her get by with changing the subject before, so she decided to return the favor. "You can always count me in for a good meal."

"Great because I made reservations at Chez René in Richmond."

"That sounds fancy."

"I figured I owed you after Friday night."

Setting her paintbrush aside, Dinah pulled up on her knees and planted her hands on her hips. "I happened to have had a blast the other night, so don't ruin it for me."

"You're easily impressed," he said with a smile. "I guess you really haven't had a date in a while."

"I appreciate your rubbing it in." Though she continued their banter, inside Dinah braced herself for his questions about her dating history. The questions he didn't ask. Would they continue to tiptoe around so many subjects tonight, never quite making the commitment to step into any of them?

A brush from Alex's shoulder interrupted her thoughts. Though she was just putting the finishing touches on the *L,* she could see that he'd already reached the letter *C* and they'd met each other in the middle of the word. Whatever questions she would have liked to ask, her time had run out, at least for now.

"Looks like we're finished here." He stood up, his paintbrush in one hand and the bowl of paint in the other. "I'm going to head over to help Eli do the final touches on the dunk tank."

"Do you think it will hold water?"

"It had better or the church parking lot is going to turn into the Chestnut Grove Lake."

Alex stepped away then, and all Dinah could do was wish she could have come up with a clever remark to convince him to stay longer. He understood, even if she didn't, that they needed to stop flirting and get back to work if they were going to be ready for Saturday's carnival. She needed to get focused, too. The youth group and the other programs that the carnival supported deserved her full attention, and until Saturday, she would give it just that.

Only Saturday, after all the games were finished and the last elephant ear had been reduced to crumbs and dots of powdered sugar, would she allow her thoughts to linger on her upcoming date with Alex. Just a brief thought about it now filled her stomach with butterflies.

Those fluttering feelings were at least part of the reason she stood and took a few steps toward the dunk tank to get a better look at Alex's progress. She should have known better because as soon as she caught sight of him, as handsome with a tube of silicone caulk in his hand as he was in full firefighter gear, he was staring back at her.

The moment convinced Dinah of two things: a look from Alex Donovan was warm enough to give her a sunburn, and forgetting about her plans with Alex until Saturday night would be easier said than done.

Chapter Nine

The day of the Chestnut Grove Youth Center's new and improved fall carnival couldn't have been more perfect in Dinah's opinion. God had blessed them with lovely fall weather all afternoon, far more suited to a sunny September Saturday than one twenty days into October.

The church parking lot had been transformed into an amusement park with everything from a Tilt-A-Whirl and Ferris wheel to an inflated bounce room and a tall slide that children rode using burlap bags as flying carpets.

The glitter-covered fairy-tale castle that stood in the center of those midway rides might have appeared out of place to some, but to Dinah, it was the perfect blend of past and present. The castle had been the centerpiece for last year's fairy-tale theme, and the children would likely enjoy the chance to play in it again.

Dinah poured more kernels into the industrial popcorn popper, sick enough of the smell that it would be spring before she would crave movie popcorn again.

At least she hadn't been stuck with cotton candy duty though. Newlyweds Andrew and Miranda Jones Noble were the unfortunate souls who'd drawn the latest cotton candy shift, and already they wore as much of the fluffy blue confection in their hair as they were whipping around paperboard wands and stuffing in plastic bags.

For the third time in the last fifteen minutes, Miranda's seven-year-old son crept past Dinah on his way to try to swipe a taste of the fluff.

"Daniel, if you don't get out of here right this instant, you won't be going on any more rides the rest of the afternoon."

Miranda's voice sounded stern, but she grinned at her husband when he passed Daniel a wand of candy and tucked the appropriate number of tickets in the collection container.

Adjusting her sanitary gloves, Dinah glanced back at her machine as the kernels popped in the little tray at the top, spilling over and beginning to refill the bottom of the glass container. With her large metal scoop, she filled more of the red-and-white popcorn boxes that would be gone again as soon as another wave of children passed by the food booth on their way to the carnival games.

"Popcorn. Get your hot popcorn."

The words were barely out of Dinah's mouth when Eric Pellegrino and his new wife, Samantha, stepped to the front of the line.

"Two boxes, please," Samantha said.

"Two boxes? Isn't one enough?" Eric asked her, lifting his brow.

"I need my own," she said to both Eric and Dinah, grinning. Leaning forward, she spoke to Dinah in a conspiratorial whisper. "Whenever I share with him, he eats the whole box."

Eric looked offended. "I do not." But then he shrugged. "Well, not all of it."

"Have you heard any word on the adoption?" Dinah asked. Eric had been in the process of adopting two brothers from Africa when he'd fallen in love with and married Samantha.

Samantha shook her head. "You know what a lot of red tape foreign adoptions can be. It's taking a while, but Amani and Matunde are going to be with us eventually. I just know it."

The two walked away, arm in arm, looking like blissful newlyweds. Both were holding their own boxes of popcorn in their free arms. Dinah couldn't help smiling after them. Samantha's past struggle with anorexia was common knowledge around Chestnut Grove since her interview on *Afternoons with Douglas Matthews,* so Dinah was pleased to see the young woman enjoying a playful attitude toward food now.

After they were out of sight, Dinah scanned the crowd for the umpteenth time in the last three hours. So many of her friends from church, the youth center and school passed by her. Others she recognized from around town—the grocery store, Starlight Diner, the post office, Winchester Park.

She would have tried to tell herself she was only looking for familiar faces as she scooped more popcorn into boxes, but she thought it best not to lie to herself anymore. She'd been looking for any sign of Alex or Brandon and Chelsea all day.

The truth was Alex had even invaded her thoughts this week while she should have been concentrating on Virginia state history and essay-writing rubrics. He'd even trespassed on her dreams when what she really needed was some good REM sleep. No matter how Dinah tried to think of something else, Alex had remained front and center in her mind. Why should she expect today to be any different?

Where was he, anyway? Had something happened with Karla's treatment, or had Alex received bad news about Mike in Iraq? She glanced again at the bake sale booth across from where she stood. Alex was on the schedule to work at that booth, but, instead, youth group members Nikki and Gina were hawking fudge brownies and pink-frosted sugar cookies like veteran hot dog vendors at a Washington Redskins game.

The two teens startled as colorful midway lights flicked on around them. The lights filled the void as the sun was already dipping behind the church building and the parking lot lamps, set on a timer, hadn't turned on yet.

Finding a lull in her concession line, Dinah slipped over to the bake sale booth just to make sure sales were running smoothly.

"Hey, you two. If you don't quit making puppy-dog eyes at all the boys, you're going to sell out too early." Dinah grinned as she selected a trio of pumpkin cookies with cream cheese icing. "You have to make this stuff last until the carnival's over at eleven."

Gina drew her eyebrows together and then had to push her glasses back up on her nose. "Why would we not want to sell out? Then we'll have made all the money we can by selling baked stuff for the center. After that we could go spend some of our own money, raising even *more* money for the center."

Because the studious brunette had a point, Dinah nodded, as she handed over a few prepurchased tickets for the cookies. "Go ahead then, but just don't steal all my customers. We won't be able to sell cold, hard popcorn."

She started away from them and then stopped, turning to speak over her shoulder. "Is there anything the two of you need before I go back? I have the walkie-talkie, so I can have Dad, Scott or Caleb bring it to you." She pointed to the buzzing gadget attached at her belt loop.

Nikki, the green-eyed blonde who had mellowed in the last year but still preferred black clothes and dark eyeliner, gave Dinah a strange smile before she answered. "Yeah, I need a date for next Friday night's football game. And could you send him with a thermos of hot chocolate?"

"I'll have Dad get right on it," Dinah said with a feigned frown. "But remember that he thinks all women should wait until they're thirty to date." *One in particular,* she could have added but didn't.

Nikki exchanged a glance with Gina and then turned back to Dinah. "You wouldn't be wondering where Mr. Donovan is, would you?"

Dinah tried to look offended. "Why do you ask that?" She raised a shoulder and then lowered it. "Sure, I wondered if he was here. We need all the volunteers we can handle today, and I did want to check on Brandon and Chelsea. Those two have been going through a tough time lately, and you know that Chelsea's been in my class for two years now, and—"

She stopped herself before she could dig an even deeper hole. For their part, the two girls continued to nod at everything she'd said, but the sides of their mouths were beginning to lift. "The lady doth protest too much, methinks," Dinah could imagine Shakespeare penning a second time on her behalf.

Dinah frowned. She'd been a minister's daughter for far too long not to realize how closely she and the rest of the Frasers were always watched. She could just imagine what stories were already making the rounds through the Chestnut Grove church community, and she and Alex hadn't had a single date without chaperones yet.

No wonder ex-boyfriend Bill had bolted when he had. Would Alex be able to handle the pressure of dating someone like her? Of course, it was too soon to wonder. They weren't even an official couple yet, but still it was hard to enjoy the newness when she couldn't help wondering when the other shoe was going to drop.

Gina chewed her lower lip, perhaps to keep from laughing. "Anyway, if you're looking for Mr. Donovan, he got recruited for a shift in the pie-throwing booth and then one in the dunk tank."

"How'd he get so privileged?"

Nikki leaned forward as if to share an important secret. "Reverend Fraser asked Mr. Donovan himself. I guess your brother couldn't make it until late in the day, and Reverend Fraser said we make more money if the kids can throw stuff at grown-ups."

Dinah nodded. Just because what her father had said was true didn't make it right for him to rope Alex into it. And why was Jonah too busy for the dirty duty, anyway? Whatever his reason, she would remember in two months when it was time to buy his Christmas present.

Wasn't it bad enough that she was a preacher's daughter? Now Alex had to endure cream pies to the face and a dunk in freezing-cold water just to have dinner with her? A cancellation probably had been placed already on her answering machine for their dinner tomorrow night.

"That's sure not the best way to recruit new church members," she answered, because the girls appeared to expect her to say something. "You're supposed to bring a pie to a visitor in your congregation, not smack him with it."

The teens laughed as she'd hoped they would.

"Mr. Donovan didn't seem to mind," Nikki told her. "Earlier he was trying to get the crowd riled up, yelling, 'Come on, buddy. Let me taste some of that cream pie.'"

Since Dinah had no trouble picturing Alex getting into the taunting role, she doubted her father pressured him into serving as a pie and dunk target. "Who was throwing the pie?"

"Brandon, of course," Gina said with a grin.

Now that, Dinah could picture, too. "Did Alex get to eat any of that pie?"

Both girls shook their heads, looking disappointed.

Dinah couldn't help chuckling as she turned back to her own booth. Her stockpile of filled popcorn boxes had all but disappeared into the hands of hungry carnival-goers. "Well, duty calls."

She crossed back to her booth and started filling boxes again. Just as she was lining the first few on the table again, the man she'd been secretly searching for all night sauntered right up to her table, his hair tousled and wet and a mischievous grin on his face.

Dinah hated to remind him of unhappy things when he looked so happy, but she had to know. "Did you hear anything from Mike?"

The smile didn't disappear as she expected it would. Alex nodded. "He called yesterday. He's fine. Apparently, there were problems with the communication satellite." He paused before he added, "You were right."

"I often am," she said with a grin. She studied his wet hair for a few seconds. "Afternoon at the beach?"

"Under the waves, anyway."

"I take it you weren't as successful in the dunk tank as you were with the pies."

"I thought they were pretty equal—" He stopped and lifted a brow. "How do you know about the pie-throwing booth?"

With a shift of her head, she indicated the girls across the way. "Your fans."

"Those two are telling you a different story because they were definitely cheering *against* me, not *for* me."

"They said Brandon missed his target with the pies."

One side of Alex's mouth lifted. "His aim improved

later. In fact, there are a couple of teenagers here with good throwing arms. I definitely prefer the banana cream to the coconut cream." He licked his lips as if he could still taste it.

"By the time I did my stint in the dunk tank, I was looking forward to the bath. Do you know how hard it is to get meringue out of your ears?"

Dinah shook her head, chuckling. "Sorry. Haven't tried that yet. I've just been here popping and popping and popping."

"And we're all so glad you have." He reached for the box of popcorn right up front. "Are these a special order, or can anyone have one?"

"Anyone with enough tickets."

Alex was already reaching for his wallet with his free hand, but he looked back at her again. "Tickets?"

"You know those things we purchase at the ticket booths and then use for all the games, rides and food booths." She pointed to the container on the edge of the table that listed the price of popcorn as two tickets and three for cotton candy, and then she indicated the ticket booth across the parking lot, the one with a line about twenty bodies deep.

"Ah, man," Alex said as he stared at the same line.

"Here. It's on me." Removing her gloves, Dinah unzipped the fanny pack at her waist and withdrew a long strip of tickets. She tore off two and pressed them into his palm. For the briefest moment, his hand closed over her fingertips, and their gazes met. The connection ended almost as quickly as it began, but it still took her breathing several seconds to return to normal.

"Thanks."

He couldn't have been as affected by her touch as she was by his because he appeared calm while he popped a handful of popcorn in his mouth and chewed without choking and collapsing to the ground.

"Eat much?" she said.

He chewed several seconds longer and then swallowed. "Not today. A few globs of pie filling weren't exactly…filling."

"Then I'm glad I could help."

"You could help me more if you could take a break right now and enjoy some of the carnival festivities. I'm not scheduled as the door guard in the bounce house for a little while."

"Uh, I don't know." Dinah turned her head to the right and left, for the first time realizing that their whole conversation had been observed by workers in her food booth as well as by the girls across the way.

Dinah had a good idea what goldfish felt like swimming around in a bowl for their crowd of spectators, and she wondered if Alex felt just as exposed. Tomorrow would only be their second date, and they were having to share their baby of a relationship with the larger church community. It was too soon.

"Shouldn't you be checking on Brandon and Chelsea?" Her question sounded feeble in her ears, but it was all she had.

Alex set the popcorn box aside and brushed off his hands. "Already done. They're both on duty at the beanbag toss for another hour."

Her thoughts raced. Sure, she wanted to spend time

with Alex. Her anticipation for their date tomorrow bordered on giddy. But tonight in front of all these people worried her.

With a quick glance at the couple behind her still painting themselves with cotton candy, she turned back to Alex and frowned. "I shouldn't really leave here. There's no one to take my place and—"

"Oh, you go on ahead, Dinah," Andrew Noble said from beside her.

Dinah startled, wondering how Andrew could have approached from behind her without her noticing. His sugary cologne alone should have been enough of a clue.

"Sure, we've got it under control," Miranda said. "Besides, you haven't had a break in hours. Just leave your walkie-talkie with us."

"What if you guys get backed up again?"

"Then one of us will come over and help," Nikki announced from the next booth over, as if she'd been a part of the conversation all along.

"Ooo-kay," Dinah said, as the last of her arguments fell away. Why was she arguing, anyway, when all she'd wanted all day was the chance to see Alex, to seize whatever chance she had to be near him?

"Well, great then. I do need a break."

Untying her apron, she tucked it and her gloves under the counter, handed off the walkie-talkie and followed Alex toward the midway rides. She still was uncertain, still wondered if this public announcement of the two of them as a couple was premature, but there was no turning back now.

Chapter Ten

Alex had already split one sugary elephant ear with Dinah and tossed a few beanbags toward, if not through, the giant clown smile when they reached the line for the Ferris wheel. Lit by thousands of clear-glass bulbs on the exterior wheel and on each spoke, the attraction towered above the church building and stood out like a beacon against the now-black sky.

When Dinah leaned her head back so far that she lost her balance, Alex pressed a hand beneath her elbow to steady her. She rewarded him with one of those glowing smiles that he'd come to recognize as her gift. Just one of many.

"Did I happen to mention my fear of heights?" Dinah glanced once more to the wheel, its laughing riders sitting with their feet dangling toward the ground. She shivered, though she wore jeans and a hooded sweat-shirt with a fleece jacket over it.

"Six or seven times minimum, at least three in front

of Chelsea and Brandon at the beanbag toss. You probably mentioned it in a few different languages, too, but I couldn't understand them all."

"Those were prayers."

"I'm sure God liked the variety of the Germanic and Romance languages." They laughed together, and for the hundredth time this week, Alex longed to draw her into his arms.

"You're sure this thing is safe?" The dubious look she had trained on the ride operator announced that she wasn't so sure.

"Of course it is. You checked the amusement company's safety record yourself, remember? It was top-notch."

"I guess."

Because she still didn't sound convinced, he reached over and patted her arm. "You know, we don't have to do this if you don't want to."

"Are you sure? You've been talking about the Ferris wheel all week. You've been telling Chelsea how amazing it's going to be."

"Chelsea's already been on it. Brandon took her on this bad boy four times in a row as soon as we got here today."

"Chelsea rode this thing?"

Dinah didn't add *and lived* to her question, but Alex figured she was thinking it. That a twenty-five-year-old woman could still be afraid of a ride that just spun like a vertical pinwheel made him want to smile, but then so did everything about Dinah Fraser.

This was a woman who got a kick out of diet soda

explosions and double dates with adolescents. She saw the world not only for what it was but also for what it could be. Then she rolled up her sleeves to do her part in the transformation.

"Sure, she rode it. Didn't the fire alarm clue you in about what a thrill-seeker my little cousin is?"

Instead of answering, Dinah looked up at the Ferris wheel again. "If Chelsea rode this scary thing, then I'm definitely up for it."

She jogged over to the rear of the ride's line and gestured for him to follow.

"Now you're sure?" he said when he caught up with her. "I thought you were scared."

"'The Lord is the stronghold of my life; of whom shall I be afraid.'" She peeked at him out of the corner of her eye. "That's from Psalm 27."

"Leave it to the preacher's daughter to have a Scripture to match any situation."

"I was trying to remember one that warned against climbing on huge wheeled contraptions that didn't go anywhere, but I came up empty."

"Maybe you'll have to ask your dad for backup on that one, but somehow I doubt even his concordances could help him there."

Dinah rolled her eyes at him, but she was still smiling as they neared the front of the line.

"You mean I'm paying again?" Already, Dinah was reaching in her fanny pack and pulling out more tickets. "First the popcorn, then the elephant ear, then the beanbag throw and now *this?*"

"Hold up and I'll get some tickets."

She gripped his arm before he could get out of line. "You know I'm kidding. I have to use these up, and I bought too many, anyway. But if I'm going to be expected to pay again tomorrow night, could you let me know ahead of time so I can get to a bank machine?"

"That's not going to happen, and you know it."

"You won't tell me ahead of time?"

He opened his mouth to clarify that he considered it the guy's responsibility to pay, but he frowned at her teasing grin. "Okay, big spender, would you pay for my ticket already?"

"The things I have to put up with."

She sighed, making a show of tearing off four tickets for her ride and another four for his. She handed them to the ride operator as they passed and then sat in the open ski-lift-style seat. Sliding in beside her, Alex watched the other man latch the door that crossed their laps, locking it from the outside.

"You see, this isn't so bad," he said as the ride lurched forward only to jerk to a stop again when the next ride car came into position for loading and unloading.

"Just a few more minutes and we'll be hurled into the black sky."

"Hurled?" He chuckled at that. "You keep talking like that and you'll have me begging to get us both off this ride."

"You mean that's all it would take?"

Because she looked up to the challenge, he shook his head. All day he'd been hoping for a minute alone with Dinah, and it looked as if this was the closest he would get. Besides, this had the added benefit of helping her conquer her fear of heights, so it was self-sacrificing in addition to being utterly selfish.

"I can't figure out how you could have gone through twenty-five years of your life without ever riding a Ferris wheel, anyway."

"I didn't have anyone to twist my arm before." With one hand, she twisted the other wrist to demonstrate. "And I didn't have any nine-year-old who could brag that she was braver than me." She paused then, as if considering. "Well, none since my little sister, Ruth, was nine."

Having seen Ruth climb into the dunk tank right after he'd pulled his wet self out, he didn't have a hard time picturing the youngest Fraser as an Evel Knievel type, but he kept that perception to himself. The only Fraser who held his interest was the one putting up a brave front while white-knuckling it on the ride's hand grip.

"Just relax. You're going to love it. And if it gets scary, I'll keep you safe. Remember, I'm a firefighter."

"You mean there's going to be a fire, too?"

Dinah started giggling, a playful, girlish sound that was different from her regular laugh. She was going to be just fine—no panic attack or anything. Good thing, because they were in a cramped space if she were to wig out or something.

"Only if you really want a fire," he told her when her laughter finally calmed.

"No, thanks. I've seen enough of the Chestnut Grove Fire Department lately."

"Anyone in particular you're getting sick of seeing?"

Her sidelong glance came with a coordinating half smile. "I don't want to mention any names."

"How polite of you."

"You'll have to tell my mom that at least one of her offspring hasn't forgotten her manners."

Every minute or so, they would lurch forward as riders in one of the cars behind them unloaded and new riders boarded, and with each lurch, they would climb nearer to the top. Because the line wasn't long right now, the operator was filling only every other car.

Each time they moved higher, the temperature seemed to drop by equal increments until Alex turned up the collar of his corduroy field jacket to cover his ears and buttoned the top button. When would he ever learn to wear a hat?

Dinah became quiet as she stared out into the sky, filled with the stars of a perfect, clear night as well as some lights of Chestnut Grove. He had to agree with her awed silence. It was the most beautiful night he could remember, and that was due in part to his breathtaking company.

"You're not really afraid of heights, are you?" he asked as the ride came to a stop with them at the top. "You just wanted to save all your tickets for cotton candy and the bake sale. Am I right?"

"Right," she answered, but her voice was tight.

"And I was worried that I didn't remember to bring a paper bag for you to breathe into in case you hyperventilated." Because her only answer was a shrug, he kept talking. "This feels like the top of the world, doesn't it?"

He chuckled then, but she didn't join him. In fact, she didn't say anything at all. "Are you okay?"

She continued to sit stiffly but still didn't answer.

"Dinah, I said, are you okay?" He didn't have to ask it again. He knew she wasn't all right. Her hands were holding that bar in a death grip, and she couldn't have sat straighter if she had a backboard attached to her back.

She nodded just as the wheel moved again, this time rolling their car backward until they sat two steps down from the top. "I'm fine as long as I don't look down." Her voice quavered on the last word.

"Then don't look down." He injected as much humor as he could into his retort, but he felt like a slime for putting her in the situation. There was nothing charitable about making her feel this uncomfortable.

"I'm sorry, Dinah. I shouldn't have forced you to come on this ride."

"Forced?" Though the rest of her didn't change much, she watched him out of her side vision and lifted an eyebrow. "When I mentioned a fear of heights, did I also tell you I have a stubborn streak a mile long? That's why my brother, Jonah's, teasing never got me on any ride more adventurous than the bumper cars."

"Why'd you do it this time?" And would this woman ever cease to intrigue him?

"I just figured it was time to conquer my fears."

Alex couldn't help smiling because her reasoning was so similar to his, even if his had been a lot more selfish.

"And because I wanted to be here. With you." She paused a long time before she said the last, but it was those final two words that made his heart thud.

"I wanted that, too."

The words were out of his mouth before he even thought to form them, and he had just as little power over his hand as it reached up to settle over one of hers that still gripped the bar. It surprised and pleased him when her grasp relaxed instead of tightened.

Curving his fingers between her thumb and forefinger, he separated her skin from the cold metal. Her fingers were just as frigid. Again, she relaxed instead of squeezing tighter. Taking his time, he turned her hand until it was palm up and laced his fingers through hers. As his fingertips brushed the delicate skin on the back of her hand, he was struck by how well their fingers fit together.

Good thing he didn't believe in silly romantic clichés or he might have had a saccharine thought that her hand had been made to fit his. Even if Alex did believe in such things, God was probably too busy to ever make fitted pieces like that.

Dinah was looking down as she said she shouldn't, but like him, she was staring at their joined hands that he'd settled on the bench seat between them. She must have looked past their hands to the point beneath the car door where she could see their dangling feet because she winced.

Either he hadn't noticed the regular progression of movement or the ride was suddenly filled to its operator's liking because this time when the ride jerked into movement, it didn't stop. They traveled backward down one side of the circle, past the entrance and exit at the bottom, forward up the other side and right over the peak before repeating the whole sequence again.

Dinah was still holding on to the safety bar with her left hand, and her grip had tightened on his hand until it was uncomfortable, but otherwise, she held her composure.

"You see, it is fun." He smiled at her as the wind caught some of the strands that had come loose from her ponytail and sent them flying across her nose.

She used the hand that had been holding on to the bar to brush them out of her face. "It doesn't stink, anyway, even if it is freezing out here."

"Come on. This is great. The wind, the speed, the weightlessness in the pit of your stomach as you drift up one side and down the other."

"Oh, I thought that was nausea."

"You're not sick, are you?"

She shook her head but turned to him and grinned. "Why? Would you care if I were?"

Alex looked from one side of their car to the other. "In a cramped place like this, I pretty much have to care."

She chuckled. "Really, I'm fine. Much better than I thought I'd be."

"It's probably the company."

"Must be."

He squeezed her hand that had finally relaxed in his.

They didn't say more; they didn't have to. Yet Alex found himself not wanting the ride to end even if the wind was blowing right through his layers of clothing. He and Dinah had other places that they needed to be later, but he wanted to stay here with Dinah, just holding hands.

The rightness of the moment terrified him in a way that an out-of-control fire never could, and yet he didn't feel the need to retreat from the flames. Maybe he should be questioning his survival instinct, but he didn't care. He just wanted to enjoy the serenity of the moment as their car passed the highest point in the ride.

The serenity that ended with a jolt and a metal-grating screech.

For several seconds, they sat stock-still as their car rocked slightly in what felt like an aftershock. Around them about a third of those clear bulbs that had flashed in the night were either blinking or had gone dark. The murmur of voices, both from those in the other cars and others on the ground, filtered through the air.

Releasing Dinah's hand, Alex leaned over the side of their car to get a look at the others below. Several riders were fidgeting in their seats, which was the only movement he could see because this ride wasn't going anywhere.

Dinah cleared her throat, drawing his attention back inside their car.

"I take it this wasn't part of the whole Ferris wheel experience you were telling me about."

"Now don't panic. It's probably just a minor break-down. I'm sure they'll have it fixed in no time." At least, that's what he hoped. He suspected the situation wouldn't be tied up so easily.

"Me? Panicking?" She shook her head hard enough to rock the car again. "No. Not at all. Not yet."

"So we have a few minutes at least until we jump for safety?"

Dinah glanced down between their knees to where their sneaker-clad feet dangled toward the ground. When she shivered again, Alex was positive it wasn't from the cold.

"At least a few minutes." She swallowed. "For right now at least, I think I'm safer up here."

"Ya think?"

"Okay, Mr. Firefighter, you know what to do in an emergency. How are you going to get us down from here?"

"Sorry, sweetie. If I'd known ahead of time, I could have brought a hose and an ax with me, but it wouldn't help to have the people on the ground spray the hose all the way up here, and I doubt you want me to hack our way down."

"Remind me to bring someone with a parachute next time."

"Duly noted. You know—" he paused until she looked over at him "—it really is kind of nice up here."

"I guess as cold, windy nights when you're stuck up in the middle of the sky go, it's not so bad."

One of those loose tendrils at her cheek blew across her nose again, and this time Alex brushed it back from her face. "Come on, Dinah. Since when are you a glass-half-empty gal? Look out there. It really is like the top of the world. Of Chestnut Grove, anyway. From this vantage point, you can look down on all of God's creation."

"You mean in the daylight, right?"

At least she was starting to get her good humor back. "Guess you'll just have to imagine it right now."

She turned her head toward him, looking suddenly

serious. "How long do you think we'll be up here? Really? Because it's going to get really cold."

"It's hard to say. The fact that so many lights are out isn't a good sign, and that screech didn't sound promising, either. If we're stuck too long, the fire department will have to bring the ladder truck to get us."

Even the shadows couldn't hide the worry on her face as she pondered those things.

"What happened to that teacher who got a kick out of the Diet Coke and Mentos experiment?"

She turned to look back at him. "How do you know about that?"

"You were so excited about it that you mentioned it that first day on the phone. I knew you were an adventurer before I ever met you."

"An adventurer with a fear of heights," she said with a sardonic laugh. "Go figure."

"We're all afraid of something, Dinah."

"Even you? You go rushing into fires when everyone else is running out."

"There are things I'm afraid of."

"Such as?"

Not knowing who I am. He wanted to say it, but he'd already stepped out of his comfort zone by admitting that anything scared him. Would it really help anyone to admit aloud the one thing that frightened him most of all?

"Trusting, probably," he said finally. It was a cop-out, and he knew it, but what he'd said was also true. He wasn't ready, wasn't sure he ever would be to face the skeletons he hadn't even known were in his family's closet.

"I sure know that one," she said with a chuckle. "I trusted you to take me on this thing, and look what happened."

As if she only realized after her witty comeback that he might be serious, she turned back to him. "Oh. Sorry."

"No need to be sorry."

Below them, a crowd had started to gather as carnival volunteers and guests realized the Ferris wheel was taking more than a lengthy break. Brandon and Chelsea weren't among them as far as Alex could tell, which was just as well since he didn't want to worry them. They had enough things to be worried about lately.

"Are you still cold?" Even as he asked it, he scooted close to her, wrapped an arm around her shoulder and drew her close to his side. "For shared-warmth purposes only."

"Of course." The way the side of her mouth lifted suggested she wasn't buying his story, yet she still relaxed against his side.

Turning his head, he closed his eyes and breathed in the honeyed scent of her hair, letting it filter through his senses and create a memory. "You know, I'm not in any hurry for them to bring us down from here."

For a second, he thought he heard her murmured agreement, but then she made a skeptical sound in her throat. "Next time you need a captive audience, particularly if it's me, would you mind making your stage on the ground?"

"I'll keep that in mind." Absently, he traced his

fingers along the curve of her shoulder again and again. "I've waited all week to be alone with you, but every night there's been a crowd everywhere we turned," he admitted. "Way up here, though, it finally feels like we're alone."

Dinah stiffened next to him, her nervousness and innocence sweet. "Why?" She stopped and cleared her throat. "Why did you want to be alone with me?"

Because of her beauty that emanated from the inside out. Because of her appealing faith, intellect and wit. Because of the connection between them he no longer could deny. He wanted to be with her for all those reasons and more, but he only said, "For this."

With the arm he had around her shoulders, he turned her toward him. His free hand went to her cheekbone, and he traced it with the side of his thumb. At first her eyes were wide, but she leaned into his hand, just as she'd allowed herself to sink into the protection of his arm. He might have been able to back away until then, but this newest act of trust propelled him forward.

Slowly, giving her plenty of time to pull away if she wished it, Alex leaned in and touched his lips to hers. It was the briefest of kisses, and yet with it, everything between them had changed. Alex swallowed, sensing that truth with a surety he hadn't felt about anything for a long time.

He should have known. If simply meeting her had reopened a dark place in his heart and if getting to know her had tempted him to trust when he'd believed the ability in him was dead, then he should have known that she would taste of sweetness, honesty and purity.

He should have understood that after kissing someone like Dinah Fraser, he would never be the same.

As he sat facing her with mere inches separating him from her lovely mouth, Dinah startled, and her eyelids fluttered open. Questions danced in her dark gaze, none of which he could answer yet, so he touched his mouth to hers once more, sinking into the pillowy softness of her lips.

Could she feel it, too? Did she feel the promises his heart made through touch when his thoughts weren't even ready to wrap around them yet? He didn't want to think just yet, didn't want to analyze the unexplainable. He only knew that if given the chance he could go on kissing Dinah Fraser like this forever.

A thunderous bang, though, made forever a very short time. It shook the Ferris wheel and reverberated in his ears. The pair jerked away from each other so quickly that their backs hit opposite sides of the car with matching thuds.

"What was that?" Dinah exclaimed, her eyes wide.

Alex shook his head, waiting for an aftershock that would send the wheel spinning off its axis, but above them, the sky exploded into thousands of lights. Thousands of red and green lights.

"The fireworks," they exclaimed in unison, both laughing so hard that tears shone in their eyes.

"I can't believe I forgot," she said.

Alex just shook his head. They must have discussed the fireworks display half a dozen times in the last week, particularly since the fire department had to be on standby for all public displays. A few minutes alone with Dinah, and he was forgetting his good sense and plenty of other things he knew to be true.

With that first pyrotechnic masterpiece dripping in ashes toward the ground, he heard a distant *pop-pop-pop,* and again the sky was alight with color. Only this time, the booms and the flashes of light just kept coming. It was egocentric to even think it, but still he couldn't help believing that the showers of light were there for the two of them.

During a pause in the noise, Dinah leaned close to his ear. "Now I've heard people say that they see fireworks at times like these, but who can say they actually started fireworks with…well…you know."

"No one accused us of being normal." But he didn't want to begin another round of the verbal banter they used to cut the tension between them, so he didn't say more. He only slipped his arm around Dinah's shoulders again and leaned his head on the back of the car so they could both watch the light show from this bird's-eye view.

"Oooh. Aaah," they repeated a few times to keep the tradition of fireworks displays. Strange how the tradition seemed superfluous when paired with a show that wasn't like any other he'd seen. From this point on, he would never be able to see another fireworks display without thinking about tonight and the lovely woman who'd shared the pictures in the sky with him.

The bangs continued, as did the popping of flowers, stars and geometric-shaped beings, born only to collapse toward the ground after their coming-out party.

Alex peeked over the side of the car, catching sight of the crowd below that had grown larger. Whether they were worried relatives and friends of the thirty or so people on the Ferris wheel or fireworks enthusiasts trying to watch the show he couldn't tell.

The angle of their car prevented him from seeing what really interested him: work on the ride's engine area. If they didn't do something soon, the riders would still be in the air until Sunday-morning services.

"I thought I heard drilling or something below us. Maybe they're going to fix this thing." Dinah peeked over her own side but then jerked back, likely remembering her own warning about not looking down. Instead, she settled her head back against Alex's side, letting him wrap his arm around her.

"Let's hope so." He hadn't heard the sounds, wasn't sure why any drilling would be necessary to fix this machine, but he hoped she was right that the technicians were finally working on it.

After several minutes in which the pauses between fireworks stretched longer than the displays themselves, the grand finale began in shooting white streams of light that exploded, one on top of the other, leaving a blanket of color and shapes before they faded to the earth.

"That was amazing." Dinah sighed, still looking up where stars continued to brighten the clear sky.

"The view from here is still just as beautiful." With his gaze, he traced her profile from her forehead, down the bridge of her nose, over the delicate ridges of her lips and over her chin.

She cleared her throat, obviously realizing that the beauty he spoke of was hers. Still she added, "God's version of pyrotechnics beats man's idea any day."

Only after they'd both become quiet did Alex hear the first siren. It didn't make sense. Both Squad Four and Engine Four were already near the church on standby because of the fireworks display.

Not only did he think it was overkill for dispatch to send a second squad and engine, or even a ladder truck, he'd hoped that it wouldn't be necessary for the department to have to respond at all. After the humiliation of Chelsea pulling the alarm, it was all he needed to have to be rescued by his coworkers.

Dinah slipped from beneath the curve of his arm and turned in the direction the siren seemed to be approaching from. "It must be a new experience for you being the rescuee instead of the rescuer."

"One I'd hoped never to experience," he mumbled.

"So I'm the one who's afraid to try new things?"

For some reason, the rescue vehicles that had seemed to be approaching the church didn't arrive at the carnival as quickly as Alex would have expected. In fact, their sirens stopped before they ever reached the church parking lot.

"Do you think they're lost?" Dinah asked.

Alex shook his head. "Something's not right, though, or they'd be here."

"Good thing this isn't a fire."

Great. Now the fire department he was proud of seemed to be taking a Sunday drive when this Saturday-night crowd was stuck on a thrill-ride that wouldn't end.

His fellow firefighters might as well have been the proverbial cops in a doughnut shop.

"I just wish they'd get here already."

Alex didn't get his wish. The engine and squad didn't show, and no more sirens blared to suggest they ever would. But even without the help, the Ferris wheel lurched forward, and their adventure came to an end.

Chapter Eleven

Detective Zach Fletcher pulled up behind Officer Steve Merritt's squad car, which had its flashers blinking and its engine running. He'd almost made it home for a peaceful night with Pilar and the kids. So close. Okay, it probably wouldn't have been all that peaceful, anyway, since Adriana and Eduardo were so hyped on cotton candy and postcarnival adrenaline that their bedtime routine would be anything but routine.

This, though—investigating unusual circumstances involving the staff of Tiny Blessings Adoption Agency and their families—was becoming downright habitual for him over the last two years. If he wasn't investigating Barnaby Harcourt's suspicious death or the abandoned baby Pilar had found on the agency doorstep or even the fire at the agency office, he was trying to track down the writers of threatening notes to agency officials or to the local newspaper reporting on the agency scandal.

Tonight was no different. Officer Merritt could easily

have handled taking this report alone. Under normal circumstances, it would have been a standard report of vandalism: a shattered windshield. The identity of the victims—Ross and Kelly Van Zandt—made the case less than normal, and the presence of another threatening letter kept it from being standard.

Zach climbed out and trudged toward the squad car, where an open door lit the interior. Kelly sat sideways in the backseat with her feet still touching the street outside the door.

Her hands resting on her rounded abdomen, Kelly looked up as he approached. "They insisted that I sit down for a few minutes. Junior here starts doing aerobics whenever I get stressed."

"There's been a lot of stress lately." Zach didn't bother posing it as a question. He knew all about the *stresses* this mother-to-be had been facing for more than two years now.

"Somebody wants to make sure that Ross drops his investigation into this newest batch of doctored birth records." Kelly moved one of her hands to her hair, worrying a few of the blond and brown strands with her fingers.

Zach followed Kelly's gaze back to her husband's SUV with a windshield that looked as if it had been on the wrong end of a baseball bat. She had to wonder to what lengths the suspect in this crime would go to prevent certain information from coming to light. Zach knew he was wondering, and he didn't like his suspicions.

"In a few months, that glass would have flown all over the baby's car seat." Again, her hands moved to her belly, suggesting her instinct to protect her unborn child.

"We're going to figure out who's doing this, Kelly."

His assurances sounded flat in his ears. He'd arrested Lindsay Morrow more than a year before for murder and for the arson of the Tiny Blessings office. They had every reason to believe this craziness would have ended with her arrest, but it was clear that someone else—or maybe a few someone elses—had something to hide.

"Then you'd better get to work, Detective." She indicated with her hand her husband and the beat cop standing next to the damaged SUV.

With a wave, he hurried over to the other men. "Okay, what do we have so far?"

"We have an opportunity for me to buy a new windshield," Ross answered in a clipped voice.

"Yeah, Ross, I'm sorry about your ride. I'm sure insurance will—" Zach stopped himself because he knew the private investigator's frustration had nothing to do with something as replaceable as a vehicle. It was about a man's need to protect his family and how emasculating it was to realize he couldn't.

"There was a note," Ross said finally.

Zach nodded. "Officer Merritt mentioned it when he called."

"Do you want to see it?" Steve Merritt held up a clear plastic bag with the note inside.

The department would compare the note to the threatening letters sent to *Richmond Gazette* reporter Jared Kierney and the one that Kelly received at the Fourth of July celebration. They would also dust the paper for fingerprints, but Zach knew already they wouldn't find anything they could use.

Whoever was writing these messages had done his homework about not getting caught. In fact, the letter looked like something right out of a TV police drama because it wasn't even written by hand but rather was formed by separate letters cut out from magazines.

Stop looking for trouble, or it just might find you.

At the end of the note was a sales brochure picture of a .40-caliber semiautomatic pistol, just like the one Zach carried in his shoulder holster. The note didn't say more; it didn't have to. The implied threat spoke as loudly as the one formed in glossy magazine lettering.

Ross's jaw visibly tightened as he stared at the note. Zach could imagine how he would feel if someone had threatened Pilar or the children.

Because it didn't help any of them for him to dwell on thoughts that could cripple any family man, Zach focused on the case at hand. "Can you tell me how long your vehicle was parked on Main Street? I'd like to get an estimated time when the crime could have occurred."

Officer Merritt answered for Ross, looking down at his notes. "That's the problem, Detective. Like about half of the people in Chestnut Grove, the Van Zandts were at the church carnival most of the day. They parked on Main and walked to the church just after lunch and didn't return again until just before the fireworks finale at around nine-thirty."

Zach nodded, taking in the information. "Well, we

can rule out the daylight hours, or someone on this street would have noticed the baseball bat or the sledge-hammer, not to mention the noise." After the last, he turned back to the young police officer. "Have you can-vassed the neighborhood in case someone heard some-thing?"

"Just ten minutes ahead of you in getting here," Office Merritt said with a shrug. "I was still on the initial interview."

"Oh, right." Zach thought for a minute. "But were there any calls to the station about loud glass-break-ing?"

The police officer shook his head. "Not as far as I've been told."

The comment, though not definitive, started the wheels in Zach's thoughts turning. "Okay, let's assume for now that no one else did call in a report. That could mean that no one was home to hear the glass shatter-ing because it would be almost impossible to do damage like that in silence."

Zach indicated the gaping hole in the middle of the windshield. "Another possibility would be that the suspect or suspects timed their vandalism to the fire-works show to cover the noise."

Officer Merritt picked up the idea and ran with it. "That would mean that the vandal knew when the fire-works display was scheduled."

Ross didn't disappoint as a former police officer and a current P.I. "And that could mean the suspect either worked with the fireworks company or was privy to its schedule."

"Or more likely yet," Kelly began, waiting for the men to turn to where she now stood, "they read the carnival schedule. It was printed in yesterday's *Richmond Gazette*."

Officer Merritt groaned, and Zach couldn't help but agree with him. Every time Zach thought he had a handle on this investigation, every time he had a good lead, something came along to shoot it down. And every time he failed to make the connections that would lead to an arrest or multiple arrests, he allowed these suspects to continue staging their campaign of fear.

Zach decided to keep his other theory to himself until he'd asked a lot more questions. For weeks, he'd been suspecting that a member or members of one of Chestnut Grove's prominent families might be responsible for this newest round of threats and crimes. The Nobles, the Harcourts, the Matthewses—they all seemed to have skeletons in their closets. What he needed to find out was whether any of their secrets involved unplanned pregnancies and cover-ups for a price.

Ross moved over to his wife and settled an arm around her waist. "You're supposed to be sitting down."

"You think I could sit with all this going on?" Kelly asked.

Zach looked back and forth between two of the people who'd sacrificed so much time and effort to right some of Barnaby Harcourt's wrongs at Tiny Blessings.

"Have you considered letting your investigation cool for a while?" Zach asked.

Both of them shook their heads emphatically.

"And let whoever's doing this win?" Kelly said.

"No, not letting them win." Zach held his hands wide in a plea for understanding. "You could put your investigation of the records on hold until our department has completed its investigation and made an arrest. Kelly, you could even begin your maternity leave a little early, letting Eric Pellegrino keep the office running for you."

Kelly waited several seconds before she answered. "Sorry. I can't."

Zach had known that answer was coming, but he had to try. "It would just be for a short while."

"What if you never make an arrest?" Ross asked for himself and his wife.

Zach had to admit Ross had a point. No matter how much effort he put into solving the case, even at the expense of his home life, there was no guarantee his efforts would pay off in an arrest, let alone a conviction.

Kelly shook her head again. "Don't you understand, Zach? These people who've had their adoption records doctored are the victims here. They don't know about the deceit or the payoffs surrounding their births or about the teenage mothers who were sometimes forced to give them up. Now if you were one of these victims, would you want us to wait another week or even a day to tell you the truth?"

There was a point in a disagreement where one side had to admit defeat, and Zach realized he'd reached it. The Van Zandts were as driven in their efforts to help these victims as he was in his mission to protect them and others. However, before he waved a white flag on the discussion and waited with them for the tow truck to arrive, he offered the best warning he could.

"You two remember how far Lindsay Morrow was willing to go to keep her husband's secrets, don't you?"

Since no one responded, Officer Merritt filled in the blank for them all. "She killed Barnaby Harcourt. And she tried to kill you, too, Kelly." Then the side of his mouth lifted grimly. "But you all already knew that."

"Yeah," Ross said.

Of course, the Van Zandts knew all about the murder of Tiny Blessings' founder. Kelly was already executive director of the agency during that dark period, and Ross had been searching for answers among those boxes of doctored records for nearly as long.

"Message received," Ross said stoically.

Zach nodded, resigned. He wished he could convince them to step back, but, like him, they were doing what they had to do. They understood the risks they were taking and considered them necessary. He didn't bother telling the couple that their dedication to their cause, though admirable, only made it harder for him and the rest of the police department to conduct their investigations.

Either way, Zach still planned to do his job, and he had every intention of bringing down whoever was threatening the people associated with Tiny Blessings. He could only hope that he got to the suspects before they made good on their threats.

"Well, was it worth the wait?" Alex indicated with a sweep of his hand their softly lit surroundings in Chez René.

"Absolutely." Dinah hadn't yet sampled a bite of the Coquilles St. Jacques, a scallop appetizer that she'd suggested as an alternative to his offer of escargots, or snails, let alone her entrée of coq au vin, and she'd already determined that this date was perfect. But that declaration had as much to do with the company as with the ambience.

Dinah allowed her gaze a slow stroll about the room, taking in the crisp, white tablecloths, round-globed candles and water goblets of delicate blown glass. She'd seen this place before in her best dreams. Either her dreams were generic or he'd done an amazing job of selecting a place that matched those candlelit imaginings.

Her gaze moved back to the man sitting across the table from her and lingered. She'd seen him wearing his casual clothes, his crisp firefighter's uniform and even all of his gear, but in this well-tailored dark suit and shirt and tie in coordinating shades of royal blue, he looked amazing. The fact didn't go unnoticed by two waitresses who'd found a lot to whisper about since they'd arrived. Alex hadn't seemed to notice the fanfare.

A soft murmur of voices and movement in the shadows suggested the presence of other patrons at the French restaurant, but as it had on the Ferris wheel, it felt as if they were the only two people in the room. Dinah realized now that they could have been in one of the long lines at Paramount's Kings Dominion Amusement Park waiting to ride the Anaconda or the Hypersonic XLC, and she would still feel as if the two of them were alone.

Because that truth made her nervous, Dinah brushed

her hands on her skirt and grasped for a topic that might lighten the mood between them. "It was nice seeing you and the children at church this morning. What did you think?"

Alex chewed and swallowed the bite of dinner roll he'd taken before he answered. "I was glad Reverend Fraser made it easy on me, preaching on how God's people prevailed, bringing down the walls of Jericho. Your dad could have made me squirm in my seat by preaching about lukewarm Christians or something."

"He saved that sermon for next week," she said with a chuckle. "He'll preach on Revelation 3:16: 'So, because you are lukewarm, and neither cold nor hot, I will spew you out of my mouth.'"

"Leave it to you to know that one." He laughed with her. "Boy, am I looking forward to that sermon."

"So why did you finally decide to try out our Sunday services, anyway?" she couldn't help asking.

"Don't you know? I was trying to get on the minister's good side since I'm dating his daughter."

"Is that all?" She couldn't decide whether to be happy or disappointed. Was it enough that he wanted to be there for her? Was his spiritual health so unimportant to her?

Her conflict must have shown in her expression because he waved away his earlier comment. "Just kidding. There are a lot of reasons we came this morning. The church members have been great to us. Eli told me to give the place a try. Brandon and Chelsea have made so many friends in the youth group, and they didn't really have a church they attended before."

He shook his head to delay her when she started to respond. "Even those were just part of the reason. The truth is that I've finally decided it's time to get involved in church again."

"I thought you already had a church home."

"Just ask the kids. My attendance record isn't exactly stellar, even since they've been living with me." He shrugged. "I thought if we found a church where we all felt comfortable, it would be easier for us to make a habit of attending every Sunday."

"Sounds reasonable." The seed of sadness in her contradicted her earlier thoughts, proving just what a self-centered woman she was. She stared down at her bread plate and concentrated on buttering a hard roll.

"I went for all the right reasons. Really. We want to be in fellowship with other Christians to do God's work. So you're not going to hold it against me that I'm enjoying the fringe benefit of spending extra time with the preacher's daughter, are you?"

Alex wore a knowing smile when she looked up at him from the table. He understood her weakness when it came to him, and he didn't seem to mind. Reaching for her hand across the table, he squeezed it but didn't release it as she expected he would.

She stared at their laced fingers. "Time with the preacher's daughter? A fringe benefit? It really doesn't matter to you, does it?"

"Why should it matter?"

"Maybe it shouldn't, but it mattered to every guy I've ever dated."

"I'm not *every guy.*"

He wasn't. That couldn't have been more obvious in her head and, surprisingly, in her heart.

For a few minutes the two of them sat in silence as the warmth between them spoke louder than any words ever could. His thumb moved back and forth across her knuckles in a gentle, mesmerizing rhythm until she could think of nothing but the wonderful feel of his touch.

When the waiter arrived with their appetizer, she hated having to let go. She had bitten into her delicious scallops when he spoke up again.

"Every guy you've dated. Were there a lot of those?"

Dinah choked, coughing into her napkin several times before she could speak. "No, not many." She was tempted to believe he might be jealous but found it safer to think he was just interested.

"My father usually intimidated them. The guys thought they had to have proper intentions. How many guys do you know who are willing to date a woman knowing they should be thinking of marriage right off the bat?"

Her breath caught as she realized what she'd just revealed.

But Alex only laughed. "Then I take it there weren't a lot of serious ones?"

"One. Bill." She cleared her throat. "I dated him for six months and thought he might be *the one*. The pressure of my family's expectations plus family gatherings, holidays and weekly Sunday services must have gotten to him because he bolted."

Bill's parting comment that committing to the preacher's daughter would be like marrying the whole church still stung as much now as it had then.

"He was an idiot."

She shrugged. "Not an idiot. Just not right for me."

"You were a much nicer person than he deserved."

She didn't know about that, but it warmed her that Alex thought so. "What about you? Did you have someone special back in Richmond?"

"Not really. I dated but no one seriously. Because I'd had in my parents a good example of a strong marriage, I didn't want to have a serious relationship until I was ready for it. A few years ago I thought it might be time, but I lost my parents, and then…" He stopped and took a drink of his water. "That was a roundabout way of answering your question, but no, there was no one in Richmond."

Dinah recognized the last as a clever attempt to lighten his comment, but she wasn't biting. "Tell me, Alex, what happened after your parents died. This is the second time you've hinted at it. Maybe it would make you feel better if you talked about it."

Alex stiffened, at once frustrated with himself for bringing it up again and relieved to be forced to face it. "I found my adoption records."

"I didn't know you were adopted."

"Until recently, that made two of us."

At first her expression registered confusion, but her face was transformed as her eyes widened. "You never knew?"

"I guess my parents didn't think I'd want to know."

"Or they couldn't find the right time to tell you."

Alex frowned at her. "This coming from the same woman who just defended the man who dumped her."

Dinah only shook her head. "Please, don't make a

joke out of this. You had to be so angry and hurt when you found out your parents had hidden the truth."

Alex wished he could say it didn't matter, that he understood, but he couldn't and he didn't. "What can you say about finding out something that made you question your family, your faith, everything?"

She drew her eyebrows together, appearing to ponder what he'd said. "I can see how it would make you question your parents, but why did you question your faith?"

"Just as they were the best example I had of a lasting relationship, my parents were my best examples of true Christians. If they could have such a strong faith and then think it was all right to keep a secret like that—a lie of omission as far as I'm concerned—then maybe everything I believed—"

"Oh, Alex, you didn't forget, did you?"

He frowned at her. "Forget what?"

"That churches are full of sinners—your parents included. From the pulpit to the rear doors to the office where the trustees count the offering, churches are chock-full of sinners. Only God's grace makes the difference."

"I know that." And he did in his head. It just wasn't as easy to accept in his heart where his anger was entrenched better than a platoon of soldiers in a weeklong battle. "I realize my parents were human. I just wish they'd told me. Earlier. Later. Sometime."

Before he'd held her hand across the table, and now Dinah reached for his. "I'm sure they wanted to tell you. Maybe they didn't know how."

"They should have found a way instead of leaving me to find the adoption papers after they were gone."

She pressed her thumb gently into the back of his hand, offering support. "You're right. They should have. Now you have to decide if you can forgive them."

"You make it sound so simple."

"It's anything but simple. Still, you have to find a way to put the issue to rest, or you'll never find peace."

"That's just the thing. I can't. Put it to rest, that is. Ross Van Zandt, a private investigator working with Tiny Blessings Adoption Agency, informed me that my adoption records were some of the ones that Barnaby Harcourt falsified."

"Oh, Alex," she said, squeezing his hand. "That had to feel like another betrayal. Not only the parents who loved and raised you and the people who gave you life but now those who doctored the records, as well."

Alex could only stare at her. She'd so succinctly described feelings he hadn't been able to put into words. More than that, she'd understood him when he'd felt for so long that no one ever would. Lately, he'd been trying to compartmentalize his reactions to and feelings for Dinah, but it was becoming harder to tuck them into their appropriate places when they loomed large all around him.

"If Ross contacted you, does that mean he has answers for you or just that he knows the documents were falsified?"

He drew his hand out of her grasp as the waiter delivered their entrées. Though the Chicken Cordon Bleu on his plate looked delicious, he found he wasn't ready to sample it. He waited until the waiter backed away from the table to answer her question.

"Ross has the name of the woman who probably is my birth mother. It could be a maiden name, and he hasn't located her or anything, but he has a name to start with."

Dinah took her time chewing a bite of her chicken, swallowing and wiping her mouth with a napkin before she spoke again. "You told him not to go any further, didn't you?"

Alex couldn't keep the surprise off his face. "How did you know?"

"It makes sense." She shrugged, stirring the sauce on her plate. "You've hardly had time to digest the fact that your adoptive parents kept the truth from you, and now you're expected to jump at the chance to find the woman who was willing to give you away?"

"Ross sure didn't see it that way." He stared again at the woman who easily viewed the situation through his eyes.

"You'll have to forgive Ross. His work is all about puzzles and solutions, and he's been working so hard to help Kelly repair the damage at Tiny Blessings." She held her hands wide. "It's probably hard for him to see each of those files as an individual set of lives when he's so focused on the puzzle."

"I still can't believe someone bashed in his windshield last night."

"And we thought those sirens were for us." She chuckled over the irony before becoming serious again. "I'm worried about Ross and Kelly, though. With those threatening letters and now this, I worry about the risks they're taking to find the answers for Tiny Blessings."

"That must make Ross even more frustrated with people like me who aren't interested in the truth of their birth." He shifted in his seat, settling his forearms on the edge of the table. "He offered to search for my birth mother, and I told him I would think about it, but I don't know if I'll ever want to go there."

"You don't have to, either." The vehemence in her voice must have surprised her as much as it had him because her hand flicked to her mouth. She coughed into her fist before trying again. "It's up to you. It's your life. If you choose never to search for your birth mother, then you don't have to."

"I'm glad to have your permission, anyway."

He winked at her to let her know he was joking. In truth, he didn't know what to make of this woman who sensed his feelings and even seemed to feel anger on his behalf. Her empathy touched him in a way he couldn't explain.

Dinah put her fork aside. "You've had a lot to deal with lately, from caring for Chelsea and Brandon to worrying about Karla and Mike and now this."

"Let's not forget a rash of false alarms at the local elementary school." The side of his mouth lifted.

"No, we can't forget that." She smiled back at him. "Anyway, thanks for sharing your secret with me."

He tilted his head, studying her. He hadn't confessed his need to keep the information regarding his adoption to himself or his strange feeling that he was an imposter in his own life, but again she seemed to understand. "I'm glad I told you."

He was glad and relieved. Telling Dinah felt like

taking a step forward when he'd been in what seemed an interminable pause since he'd discovered the truth about his birth.

Their conversation moved on to more pleasant subjects—to Dinah's announcement of how much more settled Chelsea had been in school and to Alex's report on Karla's improving health—and then on to memories from the carnival the night before. Neither mentioned their kisses or the literal and figurative fireworks that followed, but it was on Alex's mind, and he sensed it was on hers, as well.

In the glow of candlelight, Alex continued to watch Dinah as she spoke and as she laughed, her eyes crinkling at the sides. He'd thought she was attractive the day he'd met her, but she'd never looked more beautiful than she did that night. Something had changed about Dinah, but he suspected it wasn't anything specific in the woman herself but how he saw her. He had the disconcerting suspicion that he was seeing her not as the woman who'd intrigued him the last few weeks but as the woman he loved.

Chapter Twelve

Dinah stared up into the dark sky, striped with white stratus clouds, and breathed in the cool breeze coming off the Kanawha Canal as she walked alongside Alex on Richmond's Canal Walk. The well-lit walkway led all the way from Fifth Street to Seventeenth Street past park areas, grandstands, restaurants and shops.

Though this late on a Sunday evening most of those shops and restaurants were closed and this far into the fall season the outdoor dining tables and umbrellas were stored away, the walk was still romantic as the moonlight danced in the dark water of the canal.

"I'm glad you suggested this place." She glanced at another couple, arms linked, walking a hundred yards or so ahead of them.

"Yeah, me, too." He was looking up at the same sky that only last night had been packed with visible stars. Tonight, only a few insistent spots of light broke through the maze of clouds.

"I've only been here with my parents…and in daylight." She didn't mention that an outing with her parents tended to trim the romance out of any situation, but she figured he caught her drift.

A chilling wind brushed her skin then, proving how little insulation her brand-new black peacoat provided from the cold, but Dinah only fastened the buttons at her throat and continued walking. Even the cold couldn't bother her on this night. It was near perfect just because she and Alex were there together. Alex moved the evening one step closer to perfection by taking her hand.

When Alex stopped her and gently turned her to face him, her eyes fluttered closed. Then he grabbed her second hand.

"No gloves again? You have to be freezing."

"It's a new coat," she said with an embarrassed shrug. At least she hadn't puckered, but she didn't delude herself that he'd missed what she was thinking. "I haven't found a good pair of matching gloves for it yet."

"And we all know how important it is to coordinate." He was kidding her, but he still gave her hands a brisk rub between his thumbs and fingers, restoring much-needed circulation.

He released her hands and dipped into the pockets of his topcoat, pulling out a pair of leather gloves. "Here. Put these on."

"Thanks." She took a glove, pulling it on her right hand, and he helped her on with the left. "But aren't you cold?"

Letting her turn back until they were side by side again, he took one of those gloved hands in his, awkwardly lacing their fingers together, and started walking again. "No, this is just fine."

"Okay then." She grinned into the darkness.

For a long time, neither of them spoke as they walked, the whoosh of the water and the rumble of far-off vehicles the only sounds filling the night. Their joined hands moved in a steady rhythm, timing with Dinah's pulse yet sharing no secrets of the expanding feelings in her heart.

She was warm now, all right, and it had nothing to do with Alex's gloves. And had everything to do with Alex himself. Could he be the man God had intended for her all along? Had God known that Alex would be entering the picture even before Bill had exited it?

She shouldn't have been entertaining those thoughts, her good sense warned. It was too soon, too much of a risk. She was naive and vulnerable. Daring to hope was dangerous when her own history told her it was a mistake.

Still, Alex broke through her best defenses, with his silly jokes, his half grins and his gazes that were so intense he had to see straight to her heart. What would he see if he examined it closely? Would the wave of emotions be enough to send him running in the opposite direction?

But nothing frightened Alex Donovan, except maybe facing his own past, and no one would blame him for being cautious there. He wasn't afraid of a three-alarm fire, a crowd of heckling children or, more intimidating than either of those, her father in Papa Bear mode.

Dinah smiled as she thought of how Alex had earned her father's respect. Alex had joked tonight that he'd wanted to get on the minister's good side since he was *dating his daughter.* He'd said it as if it was an ongoing thing rather than something limited to one chaperoned pizza outing and a single, private dinner date. He'd made no promises for anything beyond that, though he was so wonderful that Dinah was tempted to ask.

No wonder her mother and Ruth had become charter members of Alex's fan club along with Dinah as the founding member. She had admired him from the first, his heroic qualities as apparent in his attentive care for his cousin's children as in his job protecting the public. His good looks had appealed to her in the beginning, but it was his kindness, compassion and humor that kept drawing her closer.

"It's colder than it was last night." He paused before adding, "Except on the Ferris wheel."

"Yes, it is." Dinah swallowed as images of their ride and their kisses flooded her thoughts again. He'd intended on invoking those thoughts, she knew. She didn't know, though, why he wanted her to remember and what last evening's events had meant to him.

Alex's kiss had felt like a promise made without words, and she'd willingly accepted its gift. But had her feelings been one-sided? Had Alex believed that a kiss was just a kiss, and would that be enough for her if he did?

As she was gathering up the courage to ask him, Alex stopped again near a park area, turned her to face him and covered her lips with his own. He didn't rush but lingered there, testing and coaxing a reaction from her, until her arms clasped at the back of his neck, bulky gloves and all.

She needed to pull away, to put words to an expression that could mean everything or nothing, but couldn't seem to let go. She felt so safe in his arms. His presence was solid when all else around her seemed fluid.

When he pulled back, it was only far enough that he could still grip her forearms and rest his forehead against hers. "I've wanted to do that all night."

She shivered, only partly from the loss of the warmth she'd found in his arms. Now wasn't the time to tell him she'd had similar thoughts all through dinner and after. "But why?"

"Why what—" he began but stopped himself as realization must have settled. "Why would I want to kiss you? Have you ever taken a look in the mirror?" He chuckled at his own joke at first, but then his gaze narrowed. "I don't understand. What are you asking?"

He stiffened and took a step back, his hands falling to his sides.

As she stared down at his hands, already missing his touch, she struggled to put her worries into words. "Over these past few weeks, we've become friends— good friends—outside of our concern for Chelsea and Brandon."

"That's a good thing, right?"

She nodded, frustrated that she couldn't get her point across the way she wanted. "As we've gotten to know each other better, our relationship has become more than friendship. At least on my part."

He was smiling now, but he crossed his arms over his chest, waiting for her to finish.

Dinah cleared her throat to try again. She considered covering her face with her hands as she spoke, but she stared at the toes of her pumps instead. "About the kiss…or…um…I guess…kisses…plural. I don't know what they meant. Or if they were intended to mean anything at all. I just can't be casual about—"

"About kissing?"

At Alex's question, Dinah looked up sharply. "You're not making this any easier, you know."

"I'm sorry. You just took me by surprise. Or the irony did."

Instead of asking what irony, Dinah planted her hands on her hips and waited for an explanation. Whatever he had to say couldn't be any more mortifying than what she'd already said herself.

Alex took his cue. "You're right, Dinah. We have more than friendship going on here. On my end, too. You've become very important to me."

He paused long enough to step closer and take both of her hands again. "Don't you see? Kissing you could be a lot of things. Exciting. Terrifying. Telling. But it could never be casual." He shook his head. "Not for me."

She didn't know which of them moved first, but she was back in his arms again, her heart so close to his, and his hands combing gently through her hair. When he tilted his head so he could touch his lips to hers, she smiled against his mouth. There was a promise in his kiss, and hope and joy.

When he ended the kiss and backed away from her,

Dinah felt breathless, her heart hammering in her chest. Her lips tingled, and the skin on her chin had become sensitive, abraded by his five o'clock shadow.

Alex's breath sounded labored, as well, as he rested his cheek against hers. Turning her head, she kissed his cheek, hoping he would kiss her lips once more.

Instead, he rested his hands on her shoulders and took a step back from her again, lowering his hands to his sides. He must have read the confusion in her eyes because he tilted his head to the side and smiled.

"Take pity on a poor guy, will you? I'm trying to be a gentleman here, and in order to do that, I'm going to have to take you home right now."

Her cheeks burned. "Oh. Sorry. I didn't mean…" She let her words fall away, feeling like a silly ingenue instead of a secure woman of twenty-five. She was out of her element here with feelings that were too new, too powerful.

"Why would you be sorry? I'm not. God made you this way—stunning, amazing, effortlessly alluring."

He shifted and cleared his throat but didn't say more, as if he'd said too much already. Taking her hand and tucking it in the curve of his arm over his coat, he started back for the car.

As their steps fell into a rhythm, Dinah realized Alex hadn't answered her question. Sure, he'd responded to the question she'd asked aloud about what their kisses meant, but she didn't have an answer to the more important, unspoken one: what were his intentions? She hated that she felt like another chip off the old Fraser block, but it was killing her not knowing what Alex felt.

Maybe it was too soon to define their relationship, anyway. He hadn't stated for the record that he was looking for a wife or a fiancée or even a steady girlfriend, but the things he had said were encouraging. He'd told her he thought of them as more than friends, that he'd visited her church partly because of her and even that kissing her wasn't casual for him. He'd said she'd become important to him. Wasn't that enough for now?

Strange, important didn't begin to describe what he'd come to mean to her over these past weeks. In her thoughts, he'd started out as the heroic bachelor, and he'd transformed into her definition of masculinity, of kindness, of gallantry. Just now he'd proven himself the kind of Christian gentleman she was privileged to know as he guided them both away from temptation.

Somewhere along the way, her feelings for him had become more than admiration. Those feelings had turned tender, though she didn't know if she dared call it love. Her chest tightened at just the thought of it, whether with fear or certainty she wasn't sure. She was convinced of one thing, though: the prospect of a world without Alex Donovan in it was too dark to imagine.

When they reached the car, Alex opened the door for her and closed it once she was inside.

"Are you warm enough?" he asked after he'd adjusted the heat.

"I'm fine. Thanks."

But was she fine? Her feelings were in a jumble, and her thoughts were racing too quickly to control. Did she want a future with Alex? Was she ready to risk the pain of loss for the chance of a life with him?

Her mind told her to be wary, but her heart longed to throw caution to the wind. If love was this exciting and terrifying feeling of weightlessness that she experienced every time Alex looked at her, spoke to her or touched her, it didn't matter whether her plans were cautious or reckless. For her heart, it was already too late.

Alex unlocked the front door of his house Wednesday night and shouldered it open, balancing a paper grocery bag in one arm and a stack of junk mail and a copy of the *Richmond Gazette* in the other. He'd made it through the door, managing to juggle it all, before he tripped on the hall carpet and the mail went scattering across the floor in one direction and cans of green beans and spicy chili rolling in the other. It was just another mishap in a day filled with minor agitations that bugged him more than they would have any other day.

"Oh, for the love of—" He stopped himself before he said something he would regret and the children could use as blackmail in the coming days. There wasn't any real damage, anyway. The eggs and glass jar of Great Northern beans were in the bags that Brandon carried.

As if on cue, Brandon traipsed through the door behind him, two plastic-handle grocery bags hooked over his arms. Alex stiffened at Brandon's raised eyebrow and frown. Now that the excitement of the carnival was over and they'd cut back their time at the youth center, the boy was right back to his surly self.

"Chelsea, could you help me out here?"

"Sure, Uncle Alex." The last one through the door, Chelsea dumped her coat and shoes and plopped on the floor, stacking the bills and junk mail in a neat pile, arranged by size.

Even the child's help annoyed Alex, too slow and inefficient. He had the cans all picked up and in the kitchen before she could stack a single pile of mail, most of which would land in the garbage as soon as he flipped through it, anyway.

"Here, Uncle Alex."

Chelsea grinned up at him as she handed him the mail, her childlike willingness to please only making him feel guiltier. Alex pasted on a smile and thanked her for her help. She didn't deserve to have to deal with his crummy attitude.

He wished he didn't know from where his discontent had originated, but he chose not to lie to himself. He'd felt *off* all week. He could have blamed it on Mike's call from Iraq Monday to say his emergency leave had been delayed yet again or even the news Tuesday night that Karla had developed an infection, causing another setback in her chemotherapy.

Each was a big enough worry on its own but hardly new in his life. He spent nearly every day waiting for bad news. Anyway, his discontent had begun before he'd learned either of those pieces of news, and he knew it. From the moment Sunday night when he'd realized Dinah's feelings might be as serious as his, he'd had this sick feeling that a relationship between them would be a mistake.

It didn't make any sense. He'd looked forward to that night alone with her for more than a week, and he'd loved every minute of it—watching her, listening to her laugh, kissing her and cradling her in his arms. Her tentative admissions about kissing and about her feelings for him had been sweet and humbling.

So why, when he should have been thanking God for blessing him with an amazing woman like Dinah, was he experiencing this strange ennui? Didn't he want to be with her? He shook his head to clear his thoughts. Of course he did. So much his heart ached. But he wondered if being with *him* was in Dinah's best interests.

He was only now beginning to realize how deeply the discovery of his adoption records had affected him. If he didn't know who he was, how could he make an honest effort at a relationship? He shouldn't have allowed things to develop between Dinah and him. He was in no position to be entrusted with her heart.

Dinah deserved a man who could focus on her needs exclusively, and he couldn't even give her a fair share of his time. Not right now. Chelsea and Brandon needed him as much as ever, and he couldn't foresee that changing anytime soon.

If those weren't enough, there were still other reasons why he was questioning the advisability of a relationship with Dinah, at least for the time being. She was from a family with a strong faith, and he was one of those guys who constantly questioned his. Even his dangerous job made him a risky choice for her. Every time he entered a building—"buddy system" or not—he took a chance that he wouldn't come out alive.

Dinah deserved better than all of those things. She deserved better than him.

With the mail in his hand, Alex returned to the kitchen and made quick work of disposing of it before unpacking the groceries. Usually, he would have asked Chelsea and Brandon to help, but this time he was glad they'd slipped away to their rooms, leaving him to make dinner in peace.

After browning a pound of hamburger with some chopped onions, stirring in a can of enchilada sauce and filling and rolling the tortillas, he put the baking dish in the oven to melt the cheddar. At least there wouldn't be any complaints about dinner tonight since enchiladas were one of the children's favorites. His patience was thin enough already, and he didn't need to test his limit.

Waiting for the mixture to bake, Alex turned to his copy of the *Richmond Gazette* on the countertop. For once, he hoped there would be some positive articles to accompany the gloom and doom usually dominating the news.

His gaze moved over the top half of page one, from the top story on the newest case of political corruption in Washington, D.C., to an article printed down the right column about the armed robbery of a Richmond bank. Barely scanning both, he flipped open the paper so he could see the bottom half of the front page. The headline just beneath the fold stopped him cold: Victims and Tiny Blessings: Agency Adoptee Finds Closure in Meeting Birth Family.

For several seconds, Alex could only stare at the headline before he could bring himself to read the article about Ben Cavanaugh meeting his birth family. It was the story Ross had told him about during his visit to the firehouse—about another man whose birth records had been falsified—but it could easily have been a story about Alex. As much as the term *victim* grated on Alex, he acknowledged that he and Ben shared that unfortunate history.

Ben described in glowing terms his meeting with his half siblings and his biological mother's husband, but there was sadness to the story of a discovery made too late. Alex's stomach clenched at the realization that if he ever decided to locate his birth mother, he could be too late, as well. Maybe he already was.

"I thought I knew who I was, but there was this whole part of me that I knew nothing about," Ben was quoted as saying in the article. "Some of my questions were so deep inside me that I didn't even realize I needed to ask them."

The last Alex reread several times, realization dawning like the sun burning off layers of fog. Could that be it? Were his own questions the reasons for his disquiet, for his inability to get on with his life? That solution sounded too simple to trust, and because he had gotten out of the habit of trusting, he didn't.

He folded the newspaper and pulled out the dishes to set the table. That should have been Brandon's chore tonight, but Alex wasn't in the mood to argue with him. He'd had enough of a battle on his hands when he'd insisted that Chelsea and Brandon help him rake leaves Tuesday night.

Just as the buzzer on the oven went off, the phone

rang. Alex flicked off the timer and crossed to the wall phone to check the caller ID display.

Dinah. Again.

She'd phoned Tuesday, too, but they'd been outside and missed it. Maybe she was wondering why he hadn't called Monday as he'd said he would, especially when he'd mentioned something about possibly having her over for dinner sometime this week.

This time he nearly picked up the receiver, wanting to hear her voice and share her optimism that all was well in the world. Still, at the second ring, Alex continued to stare at the phone. He reasoned that it hadn't been an official date, just a suggestion, but that didn't stop him from feeling guilty about it.

With a start, he realized their relationship would have a pattern from this point on. She would be patient and understanding. He would be too needy and would fail to give her anything she deserved. She would forgive him and continue to be understanding.

He would make them both miserable.

Chelsea's door came open as the phone rang a third time. "Uncle Alex, the phone is ringing."

"I got it," he called back as the door closed again.

The phone rang once more and flicked to voice mail. He swallowed and turned away from the phone. This was just as well. If he stepped away now, maybe he could spare Dinah some pain later.

Turning back to the oven, he used the mitt to remove the baking pan, setting it on a hot pad on the table.

"Brandon. Chelsea. Dinner," he called out as he did most nights.

As usual one bedroom door yanked open immediately, while the other he expected to take a while. This behavior was one of Brandon's attempts for control in the power struggle that had stopped for a while and had begun again with a vengeance.

"Be right there," Chelsea answered, running down the hall to wash her hands in the bathroom.

"Brandon," Alex called out once more, but he didn't get an answer or even the sound of an opening door as his response.

"I'm not in the mood for this," Alex grumbled as he started down the hall. The boy had picked the wrong night to mess with him, and he would soon regret his mistake.

At the door, Alex forced himself to knock, though he was tempted to throw back the door. No answer. Alex took the deep breath that he knew Karla and Mike would have been proud of him for doing. Parenting wasn't for the faint of heart, that was for sure.

He knocked again, this time with more insistence. "Brandon, I said it's time for dinner."

Nothing. Nada.

Okay, he was trying to be patient, trying to give the kid some space, but every man had his limit. "I'm coming in." He started to turn the knob, but it was locked, the way Brandon usually kept it even though there was a key perched at the top of each bedroom door frame. Reaching up, Alex grabbed a key and unlocked the door.

He felt the breeze through the cracked door before he saw the open window, its curtains flapping in the wind.

Besides the mess that had become another matter of contention between him and the boy, the room was empty.

"Uncle Alex, the window's open."

Until Chelsea piped up, he hadn't realized she stood behind him. He turned to find her looking in the room curiously.

"Where's Brandon?"

That's what I'd like to know. "I'm sure he had to go somewhere really quick, and he'll be right back." It was all Alex could come up with without worrying her.

"Oh."

She accepted it so easily that Alex could only hope he was right. He figured he had the first part right, anyway. The *somewhere* Brandon had gone was probably to *hang out* with some of those friends Alex had hoped to avoid by involving the children in the Chestnut Grove Youth Center. In this parenting initiative at least, he had failed.

"Are we going to eat without him?"

Alex smiled at that. Children were nothing if not self-absorbed. "I think I'll wait for Brandon, but why don't you go ahead? It's on the table. Just use that spatula to scoop an enchilada on your plate. Remember not to touch the baking pan. It's hot."

"I'll remember to say grace, too."

"Good job." At least he hadn't failed with both of these children.

Glancing at the bed that had covers and sheets piled in the center, Alex shrugged and plopped back on it, sitting up and resting his back against the wall.

Chelsea lifted an eyebrow, an expression she'd already mastered and would probably use effectively in her adulthood. "Are you sure you don't want to eat in the kitchen with me?"

Alex shook his head. "I'll be along in a few minutes. I want to wait right here for Brandon."

Chapter Thirteen

Alex didn't have to wait long. Chelsea probably hadn't even had time to gulp down her enchilada in the other room by the time that Brandon flopped headfirst through the window, catching himself with his hands. He settled to the floor and rubbed his eyes as they adjusted to the artificial light.

"Nice trip?"

Brandon's head came up with a jerk, and his eyes went wide and then narrowed again. "What are you doing in my room?"

"You're sure that's the comment you want to go with?" Alex raised a brow yet managed to keep the vein in his temple from throbbing.

The boy let himself the rest of the way through the window. "So. I went out for a minute."

"Ever heard of a door?"

"I'd have used it, but I didn't want to put up with the third degree."

Alex scooted forward on the bed until he could bend his knees and touch the floor. "That stinks for you then because you're going to get it anyway."

The boy's jaw tightened. "It wasn't any big deal."

"Where were you? At Jake's?" Alex didn't know why he even remembered the name of the boy they'd had the first battle about before, but Brandon's surprise told him he'd guessed right.

"We were just—" Brandon stopped himself as if he realized he'd been just about to give away his whereabouts. He stood up from the floor and crossed his arms in a defensive stance. "It's none of your business where I was or anything I do."

"I think it is." He stood, as well, but didn't take a step toward the boy. His thoughts were spinning. The situation was coming to a head, and he had to find a way to defuse it fast. *Lord, I need some help here.*

Suddenly remembering that his own parents used to ply him with food, he took the chance that it was a universal truth effective on teenage boys. "Look. Why don't we go out in the kitchen and have something to eat? Then we can talk." They would be talking about the consequences of disobeying and disrespecting an adult, but he chose not to mention that just yet.

"I don't want to talk. I don't have to do anything you say. You're not my father."

"But I am your guardian. As your guardian and as your cousin who cares about you—"

"You're not my cousin. You're my mother's cousin…if you can call it that."

Alex had been preparing to argue with whatever crazy notion Brandon came up with next, but the teen's comment made him stop short. "What?"

Brandon raised a brow in a look of superiority. "I don't have to do anything you say. You're not even a blood relative."

He would have known better what to do if the boy had taken a swing at him. Instinct would have kicked in, and he would have shielded himself from the blow. But for this he hadn't even known to brace himself, and so the attack hit its mark and it stung. The shock must have registered on his face because the boy glanced back at him with a smug expression.

"You didn't think I knew?" He paused long enough to turn and close the window before facing him again. "I knew."

Alex took another deep breath and mentally shoved this new discovery to the side. He couldn't think about that now, not even his assumption that Karla wouldn't share his secret with the children without his permission or his feeling of betrayal that she had.

"Well, good for you, Brandon. You know I'm adopted. A lot of people are adopted. But that doesn't have anything to do with what's going on here now."

"You didn't even know about it," Brandon said, putting in another jab.

Alex cleared his throat. He was the adult here, and he would not be baited by a fourteen-year-old, even one with excellent ammunition. "What I do know is that you sneaked out of this house, and you were caught red-handed. I don't know what else you did while you were out there, but I'll find out, and there'll be consequences for your actions."

Brandon gave him another one of those whatcha-gonna-do-about-it poses, and it grated, but Alex refused to bite.

"You seem to be acting out to get someone's attention. Okay, buddy, you have mine. I know you're angry, and I know you're scared. I want to help if you'll let me."

The boy shook his head as Alex expected he would. Alex understood that, too. Though Brandon was nearly a man physically, having earned most of his adult height, a bass voice and an excuse to shave, he was still a boy in many ways. And right now he was a boy who desperately needed his mother and father.

"I might not be a *blood relative,* but your parents have entrusted you to my care. Right now I'm all you've got."

His shoulders pulling forward as if weighted by extra gravity, Brandon hesitated long enough that Alex suspected his message must have made it past all of that defensiveness, but then he straightened again.

"You think I care," was all he said.

"You'll care while you spend every evening for the next week, from dinner on, in your bedroom," he said in a raised voice. "With the door open."

Absently, he recognized that the phone was ringing in the other room, but all Alex could think about was despite his best efforts, he'd lost his cool. Once again he wondered why Karla and Mike had considered him qualified to care for their children, and once again he guessed he must have been a last resort.

Running footsteps announcing her approach, Chelsea arrived at the bedroom doorway, wearing enchilada sauce on her sweatshirt. "Uncle Alex, it's for you."

He turned back to her, wishing he'd thought to yell out for her not to answer the phone. The last thing he needed right now was a sales pitch from a telemarketer offering great rates on a home equity line of credit, and the last thing that telemarketer probably wanted was a customer in his dour mood.

He instructed with hand motions for Chelsea to cover the mouthpiece on the phone, and then he turned back to Brandon. "You go ahead and eat. I'll take this call, and then you and I have some talking to do."

Alex hoped against hope that Brandon would take a look at his innocent little sister and let the opportunity for a nasty comeback pass just this once.

"Whatever," Brandon said.

Alex had already turned, but he didn't have to see the teen's face to know some serious eye rolling was targeted at the back of his head. He'd rolled his eyes a time or two at the adults in his life, so he decided not to worry about it.

Brandon pushed past them, and left them standing alone in his messy room.

"Here." Chelsea extended the phone to Alex with her fingers still on the mouthpiece. "It's Miss Fraser."

His stomach gripped in a tight fist. He hadn't expected her to call again tonight, when she'd only made one attempt to reach him the night before. He wasn't ready for this, another confrontation when he was still smarting from the first.

The temptation to have Chelsea offer some excuse for him was strong, but he resisted. The child had been involved enough already in his love life, and it wasn't fair to put her in this position.

He accepted the phone, covering the mouthpiece with his fingers. "Thanks. I'll take this in my room."

Chelsea started down the hall and then turned back. "Can I have some more enchiladas?"

Alex nodded. When she disappeared around the corner, he went into his room and closed the door. Only after he'd taken a seat on his bed did he finally speak into the handset. "Hey, Dinah."

"So you really haven't dropped off the face of the earth," she answered in a tone he hadn't heard before.

"Why would you say that?" His chuckle sounded forced in his ears.

"Oh, I'd been just kind of wondering how you were."

Alex frowned at the phone. She easily could have said, because he'd been avoiding her for the last three days, but it just wasn't in her to be confrontational. She probably wasn't even comfortable being the one to call him, but he'd put her in that awkward position by not calling as he'd said he would.

"Hey, sorry I haven't gotten back to you. It's been crazy around here the last few days."

"Is everything okay with Karla? She hasn't had a setback, has she?"

Her question only made him feel guiltier. Even when she had every reason to be angry with him, her first concern was still for his sick cousin. He filled her in on the details about Karla's infection and even Mike's delay. He didn't bother to tell her about his argument with Brandon because it would sound like overkill. And just another excuse.

"I'm so sorry, Alex. I'll keep you all in my prayers. You've had all of this to deal with, and here I was worrying about— Oh, forget it."

He could almost picture Dinah shaking her head, her fair skin coloring with her embarrassment, and he hated himself for being the heel who'd made her feel that way.

"I should have called," he blurted. He probably sounded like a million other guys in the history of dating, guys who should have called and, for whatever reasons, good or bad, hadn't.

"I did sort of think we'd made plans for dinner or something."

"Yeah, we did, but—I don't know. With everything that's been going on…" He let his words trail away, not sure what else to say.

"I would have understood."

Dinah was right. She would have understood or at least tried to, even if the situation wasn't crystal clear for him. He wasn't sure how to explain it to her, but he had to try.

"It's just that the other night when we were talking, I started thinking."

"Thinking. That could be a good thing." She paused before adding, "Or not."

He cleared his throat, searching for the right words. "Well, things between us seem to be developing quickly. Maybe too quickly."

For several seconds she said nothing, but when she spoke again, it was in a small voice. "I don't understand."

"It's just that the timing… Well, it isn't the best."

"I know that things have been tough for you at home with caring for Chelsea and Brandon and your worries over Karla and—"

"No, it's more than that," he said to interrupt her. "I don't even know who I am or where I'm going."

"I see."

"You do?" How could she when he'd done such a bad job of explaining himself? "Maybe…later. There are just some things I need to figure out. Brandon helped convince me of it tonight. Until I know the answers, I can't be with you. Or anyone."

Again there was a long pause. "You say that as if we had a relationship or anything more significant than a few dates. We haven't made any promises."

Her words took him aback. No, they hadn't made any promises, but he'd wanted to, and he'd suspected that she might, as well. Someday. When the time was right.

"I guess I misunderstood," he told her.

"I guess you did."

The conversation ended quickly after that with polite words but no warmth. Dinah even made a point to have him tell Chelsea she would see her at school in the morning. It was another reminder, as if he needed any more, that a boundary between them had been drawn.

Alex stared at the handset after he clicked it off, and then he dropped it on the mattress. The finality of the things they'd said pressed like a car sitting on his chest. His arms ached to hold her, but he was only clinging to air.

That he'd misinterpreted her feelings for him was just another miscalculation in a life filled with gaffes.

"It's just as well," he whispered. Though his heart disagreed, the point was moot. He'd thought he needed to step away to get his life in order. He'd gotten what he wanted but to the nth degree, and he would just have to deal with it.

Maybe later he could try again with Dinah. Maybe he could convince her that there really was something between them, something worth pursuing.

Alex shook his head to push away the thought. He couldn't think about that now. He was juggling so many issues already, and the story concerning his birth would only be one more.

But it was time.

"For everything there is a season, and a time for every matter under heaven." The verse from Ecclesiastes appeared in his thoughts. He wasn't even the Scripture-quoting type, though it was one of those things he liked about Dinah. Still, the words spoke to him now.

The time had come for him to find the answers to his questions regarding his birth. He simply couldn't go forward with a relationship—or even with his life— until he learned the truth.

Crossing to his bureau, he retrieved his wallet and pulled out Ross Van Zandt's business card. Ross had written his home number on the back. Ross had said it was okay to contact him, day or night, so Alex hoped it had been a serious offer. A glance at the bedside clock announced it was nearing Chelsea's bedtime, so he waffled on whether it was something that could wait until morning.

Haven't you waited long enough?

Alex returned to the bed, grabbed the phone that he'd tossed aside and dialed.

Dinah lowered the phone into its cradle but didn't immediately release the handset. When she realized her jaw had gone slack, she clamped it shut, lowering herself to sit on the bed and letting her hand fall away from the phone.

She felt numb. Though she'd suspected that Alex was pulling away when he hadn't called, to hear it with her own ears made it painfully real. For the last two days, she'd been telling herself he would have some reasonable explanation for not calling, and everything would be fine. He didn't, and it wasn't.

Dinah hated the way the backs of her eyes burned, hinting at tears she couldn't let herself cry. She hated being a silly woman who'd let a few wonderful weeks matter too much. They weren't even a couple yet. Not really.

Just as she'd told him, they'd only shared a few dates. Too bad her heart had taken the situation a lot more seriously than was wise. She hadn't lied when she'd pointed out to him that they'd made no promises, but she'd chosen not to say that her heart had made some commitments all on its own.

Alex had offered all kinds of reasons for backing

away from her. Though they'd all sounded like excuses to her, she wondered if, perhaps, he hadn't mentioned the biggest excuse at all.

No, he hadn't come out and said it, but she suspected all the same that this was about her family.

It felt like some cruel déjà vu from her romantic history. He'd once indicated that it didn't matter to him that she was a preacher's daughter, or at least he'd asked why it should have mattered. Now it was clear that it had.

At once, snippets of their conversation from Sunday night drifted into her thoughts.

"What were you thinking?" she said in a low voice that wavered more than she would have liked.

At the time, sharing those stories about Bill and the other mishaps of her dating history had seemed so natural. She'd wanted him to really know her, to understand her. When he'd returned the favor by sharing stories of his own past, it had felt like such a gift. They'd connected on a deeper, more personal level, or at least so she'd thought.

Why hadn't she considered what Alex might read into her sharing those stories? Why hadn't she realized that he might think she was giving him some sort of subliminal message to warn him he'd better have honorable intentions? Had he thought that? Alex hadn't said so, but her instincts told her this was where his distance had stemmed from, and her history told her to trust her instincts.

Besides, if he had come to that conclusion, would he have been right? Just a little bit? She couldn't deny the truth in it, here in the privacy of her own thoughts.

Though their relationship had been new and as fragile as a seedling, she'd secretly prayed for deep roots. For permanence.

With a moan of frustration, Dinah flopped back on the bed and covered her face with her hands. She lifted her hands from her cheeks, surprised when they came away wet.

"No," she said aloud, shaking her head. She wouldn't cry, at least not more than she already had.

Dinah sat straight up in the bed, planting her hands on the mattress on either side of her. She'd had it. As sick to death as she'd become of losing yet another boyfriend because she was the minister's daughter, this time she was just as fed up with apologizing for the family she loved.

She was a Fraser. She was proud to be Reverend John and Naomi Fraser's daughter. She understood now that the role she shared with Jonah and Ruth as the preacher's children was a blessing, not a challenge, as she'd previously believed. Her parents were wonderful role models, living their faith every day of the week rather than just Sunday mornings.

Being a part of a preacher's family came with certain expectations and responsibilities, and any person marrying her would buy into both of those. Maybe she used to pity that guy, but she was so over it.

Tough toenails!

She supposed she should thank Alex. He'd helped her to realize that any man who couldn't see how wonderful the Fraser family was, who couldn't picture himself as a part of the family's important work, didn't deserve her or them. That man wouldn't be the one God intended for her. Even if he happened to be Alex.

Dinah tried to ignore the fresh stab of pain in her chest over the finality of that thought. Not the death of a relationship, really, but of the possibility, of the hope. It was all in the past now. They were in the past. He'd chosen it; she had to accept it. She couldn't let herself cling to the empty promises he'd made with words like *maybe* and *later*. He'd probably only used them to soften the blow, like a breakup where the couple promises to stay friends.

Clearly, God had other plans for her—and for him, too, though she found it difficult to think charitably today. She needed to stop thinking about the situation altogether. Instead, she should focus on the important things in her life, like her students and her church. She could probably increase her volunteer time at the youth center and even find another project at the church.

She would stay busy and let God take care of the rest. She could only hope along the way He would heal her broken heart.

Chapter Fourteen

Alex's second visitor of the day entered Station Four Friday morning even before his first guest had left. His chest tightening, Alex came to his feet behind the long table to greet the older gentleman he'd come to respect so much.

"Good morning, Reverend Fraser." He stepped around the table to offer his hand. "Is there something I can do for you?"

What he'd really wanted to ask was how Dinah was. Days without hearing from or seeing her had felt more like weeks. If there was nothing between them, then why did he feel so alone without her there?

"I don't want to interrupt," Reverend Fraser said. "I see that you have a guest."

Ross Van Zandt, who'd been sitting across from Alex and with his back to the door, turned and came up from his seat. "You go ahead, Reverend. We were all finished here, anyway." Turning back to the table, he picked up a file folder and tucked it back in his briefcase.

"Oh, hello, Ross." The two men shook hands. "I thought that was your SUV I saw outside. It looks as good as new."

"Except for a few scratches, it probably is. I thought about leaving it how it was, with a built-in fresh air vent in the front, but Kelly insisted on having a windshield."

The minister chuckled and then looked back and forth between the two younger men. "I didn't realize you two knew each other."

"A business association." Ross clutched the briefcase against his chest and his gaze darted to Alex, but he didn't add to his vague comment.

As much as he appreciated Ross shielding his privacy, Alex no longer minded sharing the secret. "My birth records were some of the ones Barnaby Harcourt buried in the walls of his house." He shrugged. "My parents adopted me through Tiny Blessings."

"It's a small world, isn't it?" Reverend Fraser used his thumb to push his glasses back on the bridge of his nose and studied the younger man. "Regarding the records, I can't decide whether to offer my congratulations or my condolences. It must have been a shock to learn about it."

"You don't know the half of it." But rather than go into all those details, he decided to focus on the present. "Anyway, I think it's a matter for celebration. Ross here just gave me the name of the woman who could be my birth mother."

"That is a blessing." With a gentle wave of his hand,

Reverend Fraser encouraged the other two men to return to the table and to sit with him. "So have you located the woman whose name is on the birth records?"

The minister addressed the question to both men, but Ross answered for them. "Oh, no, not yet. We're just starting on this file." He indicated Alex with a tilt of his head. "I just got the go-ahead."

"I had to think about it," Alex said with a shrug.

"It's always good to proceed with caution," the minister said. "Have you already determined whether the birth mother still lives in Chestnut Grove?"

"She's not in the White Pages, if that's what you mean," Ross said with a smile. "We haven't ruled out that the woman could live in this area, but these records are well over thirty years old. We're assuming it's a maiden name."

"Well, go ahead and try me."

Both of the other men looked over at him, but Alex spoke up for them this time. "Try you for what?"

"Tell me the name and pick my brain on it. Unlike you two newcomers, I'm a fixture in Chestnut Grove. Maybe I'll be able to help."

"I don't know," Ross began. "We haven't even proven the validity of the records yet. If we do find her and she is the birth mother, she still might not want to have any contact—" He stopped and shot an uncomfortable look at Alex.

If she decided not to have anything to do with him, Alex wasn't sure how he would handle it, but he decided not to go there just yet. "Ross, I think we can trust Reverend Fraser to keep the details quiet until we know for sure. He is a member of the clergy, after all."

"Hmm, I guess you're right."

Ross started to reach for his briefcase he'd set at his feet, but before he could open it, Alex withdrew the pad of sticky notes he'd stowed in his pocket. On the now-crumpled top sheet was a name, the name of the woman who might have given him life. Holding the pad in the palm of his hand, he placed it in the minister's hand.

"Cynthia Harcourt?" He pushed up his glasses and read it again.

"Don't tell me, she's your next-door neighbor, and you can call her right now," Ross said sardonically.

"That sure would make it simple, wouldn't it?" He shook his head. "No, I don't know the young woman. But her last name is certainly familiar. The Harcourts have been a powerful family in Chestnut Grove for generations."

"Kelly and I picked up on that one right away," Ross said.

Alex raised his hand. "And even I know all about the Harcourt mansion. We've been out there responding to a fire alarm. It turned out to be a false alarm."

"Did you also know that Harcourt was one of the more common surnames on the Eastern Seaboard?" Reverend Fraser's eyebrows shifted behind his glasses. "I thought not. There are a lot of Harcourt families all over Virginia, and many of them aren't related—at least not closely."

Ross held his hands wide. "So it's a needle in a haystack. My favorite type of investigation."

Alex felt like a human balloon that was being deflated. First, Dinah, and now this. What next, a fire at the shopping mall? "After all this time, now we probably won't even be able to find her." He tried not to think about how unfair it was because he'd learned a long time ago that life wasn't fair.

"No, I wouldn't say that," Reverend Fraser told him. "Not when you have Harcourts right here in town. Neal and Helene have offered to do anything they can to help make up for Barnaby's crimes. They might not know who this Cynthia Harcourt is, but it couldn't hurt to ask."

Ross grinned at both of them as he came to his feet. "It's a place to start, anyway. I'd better get going on it, so I'll leave you two to…"

With a gesture of his hand, Ross indicated the minister, who'd never told them why he'd come. Shaking both of their hands, Ross left through the side door that led first to the open vehicle bays and then to the parking lot.

When Alex turned back to John Fraser, he was smiling after Ross. "He was already planning to talk to Neal and Helene before I suggested it."

"Probably. He's a smart guy." He narrowed his gaze at the man sitting across from him. "But I don't think you came here to talk about Ross. Is this something about this year's toy drive?"

When he shook his head, Alex's stomach tightened. Had something happened to Dinah? Was she okay?

"It's about Dinah," he said as if he'd heard Alex's thoughts. "She's suffering from a broken heart. I thought I would come to the source."

The source? Alex couldn't wrap his mind around that thought, so he focused on the other thing the minister said, something equally perplexing.

"She has a broken heart?"

Reverend Fraser held his hands wide. "I usually try not to get involved in my daughter's love life, except for giving her dates the third degree—that's my privilege as a dad." He paused, smiling. "Dinah says it's hard enough getting dates when she has to bring young men home to the minister's house. But this is different."

Alex shook his head; none of what the other man was saying was making sense. "No disrespect intended, sir, but you might have misunderstood something your daughter said."

Again, Reverend Fraser smiled. "That's just it. She didn't *say* anything. But she's just been throwing herself into her work and trying to make a second career out of volunteering at church."

"From what I've seen, Dinah always gives one hundred and ten percent in both of those places."

"She knows those things won't fail her." The minister didn't say anything about the men in Dinah's past who had fallen short. "She says she's fine, but she's not fine. I hear her crying in her room at night."

"Crying?" As Alex mentally replayed that last conversation between them, he couldn't think of any reason she would have had for tears unless...

"I'm sorry, sir, but I don't understand. When I suggested we needed to slow down until I got my head on straight about finding my birth mother, she made it sound as if there wasn't anything significant between us." Again, her comment that they hadn't made any promises rang in his thoughts, and again those words smarted. "I don't understand her at all."

"Son, I probably could write a few volumes about what I don't understand about women. This time, though, I don't have to guess." He turned his hand palm up in a gesture of simplicity. "My daughter was embarrassed about her feelings and didn't want you to know you hurt her."

It made sense, and Alex could relate to the sentiment. He hadn't wanted her to know she'd hurt him, either. Did it also follow that Dinah cared as much as he did? He was still pondering that possibility when the minister spoke up again.

"You mean this break you suggested really was about your questions about your own history and nothing else?"

"Of course it was. What other reason would there be?" But as soon as he said it, that other reason became clear. "She couldn't possibly think I was pulling away because of her family, could she?" How could she believe it was anything other than his identity crisis?

"It wouldn't be unheard of," the minister said, one side of his mouth lifting.

"But I told her—"

The older man was already shaking his head. "It doesn't matter what you told her. What matters is what she heard."

"It's ridiculous. She has to know that."

"Irrational maybe. The way most of our fears are irrational." He paused as if to wait for Alex's attention before continuing. "Unlike most of us, my daughter has fears that are based on experience, and she's finding it hard to get past those."

"What do I have to do to convince her that I'm not like those other men she's known? Not like that Bill."

Instead of reacting in surprise to his revelation as he expected, Reverend Fraser smiled. "I sensed that you were different, and if Dinah will only trust her instincts, she'll realize it, too. I came here to assure you that as long as you really care about our daughter, you don't need to feel any pressure from Naomi and me."

"Then you don't have anything to worry about, either. I'm in love with your daughter." Funny, he'd never pictured himself saying words like that, and he'd certainly never expected to confess it to anyone's father before he even told her, but the words felt so natural to speak aloud. "I hope to have a future with her, but I can't move forward until I find out who I am."

"You already know who you are, even if you never find your birth mother. You're a good and honorable man, who puts others' needs ahead of his own."

"I don't know about that."

"Dinah knows. If you weren't all of those things, our wise Dinah would never have fallen in love with you."

Alex swallowed, the minister's words giving him hope. "I just hope she can wait. Until I find my answers, I don't have anything to offer her."

Resting both hands on the edge of the table, the Reverend pushed himself up to standing. "Talk to her, Alex. Let her know how you feel and that you're not going anywhere. Dinah already knows who you are.

You never know. She might even be able to help you restore your lost faith."

"How did you…"

"I've been doing God's work for a long time."

Alex was digesting that when another thought struck him. "Does Dinah know you're here?"

"Are you kidding? And give her proof I'm a meddling father?"

"So you don't want me to mention your visit when I talk to her?"

Reverend Fraser grinned, as he must have realized that Alex had said *when* and not *if.* "Why don't you wait to tell her that until, oh, about your fifth wedding anniversary?"

The October sun shone a little brighter the final Friday morning of October as Dinah wrote a list of science vocabulary on the dry-erase board in her classroom. She realized all that extra brightness might have come from inside her, but she didn't care.

After school today, she and Alex were going to meet, and she was so excited to see him again that she had to struggle to stay focused on the science chapter.

"Who can tell me a good way to remember the difference between rotation and revolution?" She glanced around the room and waited for the usual five hands to pop up with the answers, but this time she had no takers. "Come on, guys. Remember, the top?"

"Rotation spins like a top," Austin Carlyle called out from the front row, putting extra emphasis on the first *t* in *rotation* and the first letter in *top.*

"You're right, Austin. 'Rotation' is the way the earth spins, or rotates, on its axis. Next time, though, I need you to raise your hand when you have an answer."

At least he remembered her mnemonic device if he'd forgotten the classroom rules. She went on to repeat the differences between the scientific terms, hoping her students would soon remember the concepts as well as the devices they used to remember them.

But even as she went on with the lesson, her thoughts returned yet again to Alex's cryptic telephone call last night.

He'd said they had a lot to talk about, that he thought she had the wrong idea about something, that there were a few things upon which they both could agree. Thinking about those things tempted her to hope, and that much hope was rendering her useless.

"Who can tell me how many days it takes for the earth to make one full revolution around the sun?" she said, determined to stay focused.

Chelsea was the first one to lift her hand that time. Dinah couldn't help smiling at the little girl who'd come so far in these last weeks, who was returning to her old self despite all the uncertainties in her life. Together, she and Alex had helped the child reach this new place, and no matter what happened from this point on, at least Chelsea would be okay.

"Yes, Chelsea?"

"Three hundred sixty-four and a half."

"That's right. Great job."

After the science lesson, Dinah sat at her desk so she could record spelling scores in her grade book while monitoring her students as they completed their independent study work.

After a few minutes Dinah stood to announce recess when a sound she'd hoped never to hear again without prior warning erupted around them.

Another false alarm? Dinah didn't bother trying to keep her groan silent because no one could hear it, anyway.

"Okay, everyone, please line—" she began, but stopped when she realized her students were already lining up next to the door. They'd even grabbed their coats this time and were pulling on the sleeves as they stood in line. If there was one good thing that had come from their frequent "drills," it was that her students had the procedure down pat.

It didn't make any sense, though. Alex's fire safety presentations had seemed to be so successful at first. She'd really believed that the children understood now the importance of keeping everyone safe and the peril of false alarms. It broke her heart to think that one of her students, or one of anyone else's, may have missed the point.

Trying to keep her disappointment in check, she switched off the classroom light, locked the door and started toward the exit with her twenty-four students behind her. No, she amended the number to twenty-two, accounting for the two absences from the current stomach flu making the rounds at school.

As she neared the end of the hall, a strange scent invaded her senses, like plastic packaging set too close to the fireplace on Christmas morning. She had to be imagining it, she told herself, as she hurried to the open door, her students following closely behind her. This was probably just another false alarm and another humiliation for the staff.

She stepped outside into a wind so fierce it stole her breath away. In the distance, the sounds of approaching sirens battled the wind for dominance. In a matter of minutes, the engines and squads would race into the parking lot, firefighters sitting at the ready, only to confirm a false alarm and return to the station. At least she wanted to believe that was how it would happen.

Just as she'd done on each occasion before, Dinah led her class to their place by the flagpole and had her students turn back to face the building. She opened her grade book to check the names on the list against the line of students standing next to her.

"It smelled funny inside," one of the boys was saying as she passed him.

"Maybe it's a real fire," another answered.

She tried to ignore the comments that gave voice to her suspicions as she started down the list. She was only halfway down the list when something inside her stomach clenched and her skin went cold. Where was Chelsea? Anxious, she scanned the rest of the line, the students numbering only twenty-one. At once, she could picture on the board the name of the last person to use the restroom pass: Chelsea W.

It was such a strange repeat of history, and yet it didn't feel the same at all. Chelsea would never pull the alarm again; Dinah didn't doubt that for a minute. Chelsea would never want to embarrass Alex that way again. So if she was still inside, she was either too scared or too hurt to come out.

"Look, there's smoke," someone nearby announced.

"No." The word rushed out of her but the sound of the wind covered it.

Panic felt like a pair of hands gripping her throat from behind, but she shook away its hold. She had to focus. If she lost control now, she couldn't help Chelsea. She listened as the sirens drew nearer. They were close but not close enough. Chelsea needed help right now. Catching sight of Shelley Foust's row of kindergartners next to her, Dinah stepped over to her.

"Shelley, I need you to watch my class."

"Fine. But why?"

"I have to go back in."

"Dinah, you can't. It's the real thing this time."

"I have to. Chelsea's in there."

Without a look back, Dinah rushed across the parking lot to the side entry, yanked open the door and let it slam behind her. At once she was surrounded by darkness and weighted silence in the hallway. Already, the building had lost power.

Dinah became still, waiting until her eyes could adjust. The darkness wasn't complete, she discovered, as light filtered through the windows beside each classroom door. Anyway, she knew this place well, even in the dark.

Because that haze was probably smoke, she crouched to the floor and started in the direction of the third- and fourth-grade restrooms. Her eyes and nose burned. *Lord, please help Chelsea to be okay, and be with her so she isn't frightened. Amen.* After she'd finished, she realized she hadn't prayed for her own safety. God probably got the idea, anyway.

"Chelsea. Where are you?"

She heard nothing but the sound of her own voice and some mechanical-sounding pings. Staying low to the ground slowed her progress, but she continued toward the third-grade classrooms.

Only when she was almost there did she begin to second-guess herself. Just because Chelsea had been headed toward the restroom earlier didn't mean she was still there. What if she'd made it out after all—with one of the other teachers?

What if Chelsea had been outside with her class all along, and Dinah had overlooked her in a panic? What if Dinah had just made the biggest mistake of her life, and she and Chelsea would both have to pay for it?

She reached the end of the hall, not sure which way to go. Should she move forward or try to back her way out of the building? Panic welled in her throat, or maybe that was the smoke. She couldn't tell.

"Chelsea? Are you in here?" she called out again.

Nothing.

Her lungs were beginning to ache. She reached up to pull the collar of her sweater over her mouth and nose. She was just across the hall from the restroom, convinced she wouldn't find anything inside, when she heard the scream.

Chapter Fifteen

For the first time in his life, Alex hoped someone had tripped a pull station on purpose to wreak havoc. He should have been furious that Station Four had been called out for another alarm at Grove Elementary, especially after he'd made it his personal mission to ensure it wouldn't happen again, but he didn't care.

Let it be a false alarm, he repeated like a mantra. It was almost a prayer.

Still, as he crouched low in one of Engine Four's jump seats, he couldn't help willing the truck to move faster. That sixth sense he'd developed on the job—the one he'd come to trust as implicitly as he trusted his fellow firefighters—told him this just might be the real thing.

"Radio to Engine Four," came a call from the emergency radio. "Per the RP, flames and smoke are visible in the building."

Alex's breath caught, and dread welled inside him. He needed to get there, to no longer rely on the second-hand reports of the "RP," or "reporting person." He had to see for himself what was happening at Grove Elementary. Had all the false alarms made the students and staff complacent? What if someone had thought it would be fun to hide inside the building instead of going outside with his class?

Trent Gillman, the driver, who would also be the most senior firefighter on the scene and would be setting up the command structure on the ground, had already assigned one of the others to speak by cell phone with the school principal. If they could locate the building plans, they might be more likely to find the seat of the fire sooner.

As soon as they pulled into the parking lot, they could see the flames shooting from the roof. While a few of the firefighters unrolled and charged the lines, Alex jogged in the direction of the staff, looking for the custodian and the building plans the staff had located.

As he hurried past the lines of children and educators, he couldn't help scanning for the third-grade classes. Dinah would be there, Chelsea would be there, and he could be reassured that they both were safe.

Only when he reached their class, he didn't see either of them. He looked to the back of the line and followed it with his gaze to the front again. Where were they?

A young teacher he hadn't met before hurried over to him.

"You're Alex, right? I'm Shelley, Dinah's friend."

He nodded. "You don't know where—"

Without hesitation, she turned and pointed to the building. "Dinah's in there. She went after Chelsea."

The words struck him like a two-by-four to the gut. Alex felt paralyzed with a fear he'd never experienced, even in the most dangerous fires. But he'd never loved like this before, and these were two of the people he loved most in the world.

Then, as if to confirm what he already knew, the radio secured at his shoulder squawked then. "Radio to Engine Four. There's a report of two persons trapped inside the building."

"They're going to be fine." He said it as much to convince himself as to reassure the teacher.

With that, he rushed back to the firefighters charging the lines. He'd never been so tempted to run into a building without having water available—the ultimate mistake in firefighting—but he would wait, if they hurried.

"Dinah's in there, Trent. Dinah *and* Chelsea. I have to go in."

Trent started shaking his head. "I don't know, Donovan. I think you're too close to this one. You might be less help—"

"I also know more about this building than anyone else in the department. And I know where Dinah's class is." He looked frantically at the front of the building. "We're wasting time. We have to go in now."

Trent gave him the nod, and he and Cory Long joined two other firefighters in dragging the hose into the building. Together, Alex and Cory entered on their hands and knees, following the line of the wall and one of them always keeping a hand against it. Already smoke filled the hallway, stealing whatever remaining light they might have found there.

At the first intersecting hall, Alex knew to turn right and head toward the third-grade classrooms, but when they reached Dinah's class, the door was still locked. If they weren't there, where were they? Breathing in a gulp of the canned air from the SCBA only reminded him that Dinah and Chelsea had no fresh air at all. They had to find them…before it was too late.

"Dinah? Chelsea?" he called out, his words garbled by his mask. "Are you in here? Are you hurt?"

"Keep moving, Donovan," Cory told him, his voice equally distorted. "They have to be somewhere."

Just ahead of them, a ceiling beam gave way, falling to the floor with sparks spraying in all directions. Flames shot from the ceiling above them, and it was only a matter of time before the fire surrounded them. Maybe Dinah and Chelsea were already surrounded.

Dear God, please help us find them. Please, Lord. I'll do anything. Please. Before it's too late. It can't be too late. I have to have the chance to tell her I love her.

He might have said "amen" then, but a sound ahead of him—a call for help or maybe a moan of pain—had him rushing forward and dragging Cory along with him. He touched a closed door that had to be a restroom, and after checking it for heat, he pushed it open.

Under twin circles of light from his and Cory's flashlights was a room that had been reduced to a jumble of building materials and fallen debris. Another whimper drew both of their spots of light farther into the room.

In the far corner, Dinah sat, her legs trapped under a collapsed beam. She cradled an apparently unconscious Chelsea in her arms. Alex and Cory rushed forward, both trying to shoulder the beam up and off her. At first it didn't budge, and from Dinah's cries he could tell they'd only compounded her pain, but Alex wasn't about to give up easily. Not now. Not when they were this close.

Finally, the beam lifted, and they set it aside. Cory gathered Chelsea into his arms. He pulled his mask away from his face and pressed it to the child's nose and mouth.

"She still has a pulse, but she just went unconscious," Dinah said before a coughing fit struck her.

Alex touched her mouth with his gloved hand to still her. "Don't try to talk." He pulled his own mask away and shared it with the woman he loved. When the mask was back in place, he lifted her as gently as possible so as not to cause her pain, and he and Cory began retracing the line of the hose that had become their safety line back out of the building.

With her arms around his neck, Dinah leaned her head close to his ear. "I prayed for you to find us."

Alex pulled her even closer to his heart. "Good thing for you I was praying for the same thing."

Unforgiving fluorescent lights greeted Dinah when she opened her eyes either hours or weeks later. She squeezed her eyes shut and then opened them again to bring the scene into focus. The sterile setting reminded her that the paramedic had told her they were taking her to Bon Secours Richmond Community Hospital. Strange, she didn't remember anything after that.

She glanced down at the unattractive medical gown they'd dressed her in and the IV attached to her arm. It must have been a painkiller filtering through that drip because she couldn't feel her casted leg that was suspended in front of her. She hadn't known whether it was broken or not, but the cast confirmed it.

And Chelsea… Dinah's head jerked as she thought of the child who had collapsed in her arms before Alex and his friend had shown up like a two-man cavalry to carry them out of the building. Where was Chelsea now? Was she okay? Did she need her?

"Well, there she is, back among us."

At the doorway, John Fraser stood, his trademark grin as comforting as always.

"Are you going to move out of the way and let me see our daughter or not?" Naomi Fraser pushed past him and came into the room.

Reverend Fraser joined his wife by the bed. "We were wondering when you were going to finish your little nap."

"How long have I been sleeping?"

"Just a few hours, probably from the painkiller," he told her.

"Where's Chelsea? Is she okay?"

Naomi stepped forward and started brushing back Dinah's hair from her face the way she used to when Dinah was a girl. Her touch felt comforting.

"She's just fine, sweetie," Naomi told her. "She suffered some smoke inhalation, and they're keeping her in the pediatrics department overnight, but she's going to be fine."

"Because of you," her ever-supportive father said.

"Probably in spite of me." Dinah chuckled, but that only made her chest ache.

At a knock on the door, the three of them turned to see Alex standing there. He was in jeans now, and his hair looked damp.

"Well, look who's here, Dinah." Reverend Fraser stepped to Alex and shook his hand.

Alex crossed the room, grabbed one of the chairs by the wall and set it next to Dinah's bed.

"Where've you been?" she asked before she could stop herself.

"The fire, remember?" He grinned as he took a seat. "Captain Nevins insisted that I help put out the thing before I went to visit my friends at the hospital."

"How do you ever survive, working for such a tough boss?" Dinah said with a smile.

Reverend Fraser stepped closer to the bed, resting his hand on Naomi's shoulder. "Did you learn anything about the fire yet?"

"It started in the computer room. A circuit was overloaded. It appears to have been accidental. I might have found out more, but I was in a hurry to get here."

"I'm glad you're here," Dinah told him.

"It seems that about half of our church is here tonight," Reverend Fraser said.

Dinah tried to sit up higher in bed, but she couldn't manage it with her leg suspended. "Was somebody else injured? I thought everyone else got out of the fire."

Alex answered for the minister. "No other injuries. There was only one kid who took a bathroom break at a most unfortunate time and only one teacher who swooped in to save her."

Dinah's cheeks warmed, but she didn't want to think about her embarrassment now. "Then who else is here?" Dinah asked.

"Didn't you hear?" Naomi said. "Another one of the belly buddies dropped out of the club this afternoon. Pilar Fletcher is downstairs in the obstetrics ward. Little Noah, or rather not-so-little Noah, weighed in at over nine pounds."

"Zach probably won't stop grinning for a week," Reverend Fraser said, continuing the story for his wife. "The adoption for Adriana and Eduardo became final three days ago, and now Noah has decided to make an appearance."

"Their family is really blessed," Dinah said, smiling.

"They're not the only ones."

At Alex's words, Dinah glanced over at him. He was staring at her, raw emotion clear in his gaze. A knot formed in her throat, and she couldn't look away from him.

Until her father cleared his throat. "You know, I promised to say a prayer of thanksgiving with the Fletchers."

"And I'm sure they need someone to hold that new baby for them," Naomi chimed in.

With that, her parents took turns kissing Dinah's cheek and then slipped out of the room whispering something about belly buddies and their growing church. Dinah waited until they closed the door behind them before she turned back to the man she loved. The man who couldn't know how she felt.

"I was so angry with you today," he said simply, his arms crossed over his chest.

She started shaking her head. "I know. I shouldn't have gone back in for Chelsea, but I had to. I couldn't leave her inside that building, scared and maybe hurt."

"You could have both been killed."

Dinah wrung her hands together. "I know, but I—"

"But nothing." He was shaking his head, hard, as if he were trying to shake away horrible images from his mind.

"You said you were praying today when you found us."

"I never stopped praying and promising God whatever it took to make the two of you all right. I don't know what I would have done if I'd lost you both." He reached over and covered both of her hands with his.

"I don't understand. When you said you wanted to take a break, I thought you meant—"

"I think I know what you thought, but you were wrong. If you'd died today, I never would have been able to tell you that I love you."

All Dinah could do was stare. Had he really just spoken the words that she'd only dreamed he would say?

The sides of his mouth softened into a smile. "How could you not have known?"

As soon as he said it, Dinah began to wonder herself. He'd done everything he could think of to make her feel valued and precious. How could she have allowed her past to color what had been happening between them?

"We missed our meeting today after school. You said we had a lot to talk about, that you thought I had the wrong idea about something and that there were a few things we could agree upon."

"Remind me never to say anything to you that I don't want you to remember. You have a great memory."

She laughed but only ended up coughing into the shoulder of her gown again, making her chest ache.

"You'll probably have reminders for a while of why people shouldn't run into burning buildings," he told her.

"You do it all the time."

"I'm trained and properly equipped for the job."

"I promise never to do it again." When he nodded, she returned to the earlier subject. "You were going to tell me…"

He lifted one of his hands away from hers and ticked off items on his fingers. "One, we had to talk about why our relationship was so much more significant than a few dates, even if we haven't made any promises.

"Two, you had the wrong idea if you believed that my wanting to take a break had to do with *anything* but my own identity crisis. Three, you and I can agree on the fact that there's something real between us, and it would be a mistake not to pursue it."

Dinah's eyes burned more than they had in the fire, and she knew tears weren't far behind. Was she ready to tell him? Could she trust herself and him to reveal the feelings she harbored in her heart? "It sounds like you have all the answers."

"Far from it," he said with a chuckle. "But I do know that meeting you was one of the best things that's ever happened to me."

Her chest tightened, this time for reasons other than exposure to toxic smoke, and she couldn't hold back any longer. "I love you, Alex. I think I have since that first day when you came to that conference about Chelsea."

Immediately, Alex leaned over the bed rail and covered her mouth with his own. She felt warmth and a sense of rightness that she'd never experienced outside her personal prayer time.

He brushed his lips over hers once more and pulled back. "I want so much to ask you to marry me, but I don't feel as if I should until I figure out who I am. Can you wait for me until I have the matter of my adoption settled?"

Dinah started shaking her head. When he raised an eyebrow, she shifted her shoulder. "I'm afraid that offer isn't good enough."

"What do you mean?"

She smiled. "I don't mind long engagements. In fact, I'm pretty sure my daddy, the reverend, would have a coronary if I rushed into marriage, no matter how right it is. But I don't want to wait until you find answers to all your questions.

"I love you for who you are. I know your heart, and that's enough for me."

He shook his head, not convinced. "Are you sure that's what you want, even when I still have no idea how long I'll have guardianship of Brandon and Chelsea? When so much of my life is up in the air?"

"I said before that we hadn't made any promises. I *want* us to make promises."

Alex laughed as he brushed Dinah's hair back from her face just as her mother had done. "Never let it be said that I wouldn't give a lady what she wanted."

He glanced down at the floor and then up at her again. "I would get down on one knee, but I'm afraid you won't be able to see me."

"Improvise then."

He lowered the rail that separated them. When their faces were only inches apart, he smiled at her. "Dinah, I love you. Will you do me the honor of, someday soon, becoming my wife?"

"Absolutely. I thought you'd never ask."

He kissed her then, sealing the promise of two hearts. They were still kissing when the familiar sound of Reverend Fraser clearing his throat caused them to pull back with a start.

Alex pushed his chair back, but he kept his hand resting lovingly on hers.

Dinah's cheeks warmed because not only had her parents witnessed at least part or all of Alex's marriage proposal, but Brandon and Chelsea were there, too, Chelsea sitting in a wheelchair, a blanket over her lap.

"Uncle Alex and Miss Fraser are getting married," Chelsea announced with glee. She wore the gloating expression of the matchmaker who'd been right all along.

Unlike his sister, Brandon looked stricken rather than happy for them. Dinah was about to ask why when the boy rushed over to his guardian. Alex stood to face him, and the boy grabbed him for a fierce hug. When he pulled away, Alex stared at him, surprised.

"I'm so sorry. For everything." Brandon's voice cracked on the last. "Thank you for taking care of us. For bringing Chelsea and Dinah out. I can't believe we almost lost—"

He stopped then, sobbing into Alex's arms. When he pulled back again, he continued, seeming to have something important to say. "You're like a second dad to me. We don't need blood ties to connect us. We're family."

Alex hugged him again. "That's right, buddy, we're family."

Dinah smiled at all the people in the room, all of them she had come to love in so many ways. "And sometime soon, we'll all be family."

On the last evening of October, Alex sat next to Dinah at his kitchen table, with Ross and Kelly Van Zandt on the other side. He didn't realize how tightly he was holding her hand until the solitaire engagement ring he'd presented her just the night before cut into his hand.

He eased his hold and glanced at her with his side vision. She smiled and squeezed his hand, offering silent support.

"As I told you on the phone earlier," Ross began, "Reverend Fraser's suggestion to speak to Neal and Helene Harcourt about the identity of your birth mother, clearly a long shot, gave us a great lead."

"Did Neal know this Cynthia?" Dinah asked, shifting to find a comfortable position for her casted leg.

Kelly shook her head. "They were only distant relatives. But Barnaby Harcourt was fiercely proud of family history. He'd kept a book that had been printed after a huge Harcourt family reunion a few years ago. It recorded births, deaths, marriages and divorces. That book was still in the library at the Harcourt mansion."

Alex shifted in his chair. These details were all well and good, but he wanted, no, needed, to know more right now. "What did the book say?" he asked when it was apparent no one would tell him without prodding.

"We found the wedding date for Cynthia Harcourt and Lyle Roberts," Ross told him.

"Roberts? That's probably more common than even Harcourt." Frustration welled in Alex's heart. After all this time, the search for this woman was still going to be all but impossible. He sighed and used his free hand to pinch the bridge of his nose where a headache was forming.

"That's just the thing," Kelly said with a grin. "This reunion book had something else in the back—an address and telephone directory for most of the still-living family members. Including Cynthia Harcourt Roberts."

"Are you kidding?" The wheels in Alex's mind were spinning at a furious pace, possibilities and pitfalls colliding. "Have you called her? She probably moved, right?"

"Yes and no," Ross answered, his own grin contagious. "Yes, we called her. And no, she hasn't moved."

Kelly set her coffee cup aside and started to explain. "Right away, Cynthia acknowledged that as a teenager, she had given up a baby for adoption. That was thirty-four years ago. She said she let her parents and Barnaby Harcourt convince her it was the best thing for her to do in the case of her unplanned pregnancy, but she's always regretted it."

"Regretted it?" Alex hated the way his voice cracked

as he said it. He sounded more like an adolescent boy than a grown man.

Ross nodded. "She never forgave herself, even after she married and had two other daughters. They're adults now."

"Daughters?" Alex said.

"Uncle Alex, you have sisters."

Until Chelsea spoke up, Alex hadn't noticed that she and Brandon had joined the four adults in the kitchen. He didn't mind sharing this meeting with the children, especially since he'd shared details of his adoption with them these last few days. Through their conversation he'd learned that Karla hadn't told Brandon the secret before Alex was ready. The boy had only overheard Alex's conversation with his mother.

His heart beating faster, Alex asked the last, most important question. "Does she have any interest in making contact with me?"

If possible, Kelly's smile widened. "As a matter of fact, she does." She pushed a small piece of paper across the table to him. It had Cynthia's name on it, followed by a phone number. "She's waiting for your call."

"Right now?"

Kelly nodded.

"That's cool, Uncle Alex," Brandon said, turning and grabbing the wall phone.

Alex didn't allow himself to think about when Brandon had started calling him "uncle." Releasing Dinah's hand, Alex reached for the phone, probably holding it tighter than he'd squeezed her hand.

For several seconds, he stared at the phone, wondering if he should dial. Was it a blow to his adoptive parents' memory? No, he decided. He'd finally come to a place where he could honor George and Edie Donovan, understanding even if he couldn't approve of their choice not to tell him about his adoption. Should he wait until Karla was better and Mike was stateside? No, they'd tell him to go for it and be thrilled about his discovering his new family.

So what was holding him back?

"Whatever happens, we're together," Dinah said in a quiet voice.

"Yeah, Uncle Alex, we're together," Brandon chimed.

A knot formed in his throat. They were together—him, Dinah, Chelsea and Brandon.

He'd taken it for granted, but he realized now how blessed he'd been, knowing love all his life—from his adoptive family to the woman he'd chosen to share his life. Now he could be open to loving the rest of his family.

Clicking on the phone, he dialed the number in front of him. She answered on the first ring.

"Is this Cynthia…uh…Roberts?"

"Yes," she said in a shaky voice.

"This is Alex Donovan…your son."

The sob he heard through the phone line brought tears to his eyes. When she could finally speak again, she said, "My son. I've waited all my life to hear those words."

"I think it's time for us to meet."

"Past time."

From that point on, he flipped the phone on speaker

and let all of those around the table share in that moment. At first, there was some awkwardness, but soon they fell into a calm, pleasant conversation as if they were acquaintances that could soon be friends. This should have been a strange place, but it felt like coming home.

He smiled at all those sitting around him. With the help of all these people, particularly the woman who loved him for who he was, he'd learned that blood ties weren't important. What really mattered was in the heart.

* * * * *

In November, don't miss
GIVING THANKS FOR BABY
by Terri Reed,
the fifth book in
A TINY BLESSINGS TALE.

Dear Reader,

As the mother of three daughters, I am always fascinated by how hopeful and wise children can be. They see a sunny afternoon as an opportunity to play outside and a rainy day as an invitation to go puddle jumping. They waste no time on what could have been.

I love using children as characters in my stories for these reasons. Matchmaking Chelsea White in this story is just one example of how children can see possibilities that adults miss. "Out of the mouths of babes," the slightly misquoted Psalm says, but even Jesus paraphrases the Scripture in Matthew 21:16b: "Out of the mouth of babes and sucklings thou has brought perfect praise."

God gives us this joyful optimism in youth that we sometimes lose as the years go by and possibilities become disappointments. We can regain some of that hopefulness by looking at the world through the eyes of the children in our lives and listening to what they have to say.

I love hearing from readers and may be contacted through my Web site at www.danacorbit.com or by regular mail at P.O. Box 2251, Farmington Hills, MI 48333-2251.

Dana Corbit

QUESTIONS FOR DISCUSSION

1. The men in Dinah Fraser's past often had a problem with her being the preacher's daughter, but who really is most conflicted about her family? Do family members of people in church leadership positions face these challenges in real life, as well?

2. What are some of the ways that Chelsea tries to convince Alex and Dinah that they should go out on a date together?

3. For whatever reason, George and Edie Donovan never get around to telling their son that he was adopted. Do you think it is an adoptive parent's responsibility to tell? When do you think is the best time for adoptive children to learn about their birth?

4. Who are the members of the "belly buddies," and who are the first two to drop out of the club?

5. Why is Alex most worried about the students pulling fire alarms at Grove Elementary?

6. Dinah feels for Alex because he has to feel betrayed on so many levels. In what way has Alex been betrayed?

7. Why does Detective Zach Fletcher want Ross and Kelly Van Zandt to consider delaying their investigation into more files until the police investigation is completed?

8. Alex's faith is tested when he finds out that much of his life is a lie. What type of sermon is Alex grateful to Reverend Fraser for not preaching on his first Sunday visiting Chestnut Grove Community Church?

9. At first, when Ross Van Zandt approaches Alex with information regarding the discovery of his birth records, Alex doesn't want to know the identity of his birth mother. What do you think the pros and cons are for an adoptive child in locating his birth parents?

10. What are some of the ways that Brandon acts out because he's worried about his parents?